The Enchanted Shoes

...and other stories

Published in 2014 by Bounty Books,
a division of Octopus Publishing Group Ltd,
Endeavour House,
189 Shaftesbury Avenue,
London WC2H 8JY
www.octopusbooks.co.uk

An Hachette UK Company
www.hachette.co.uk
Enid Blyton ® Text copyright © 2014 Hodder & Stoughton Ltd.
Illustrations copyright © 2014 Octopus Publishing Group Ltd.
Layout copyright © 2014 Octopus Publishing Group Ltd.

Illustrated by Lesley Smith.

ISBN: 978-0-75372-651-8

A CIP catalogue record for this book is available from the
British Library.

Printed and bound by CPI Group (UK) Ltd, Croydon, CR0 4YY

CONTENTS

The
Enchanted Shoes

Once upon a time there was a boy called William, who lived with his mother at the foot of some high hills. Nobody lived up on the hills for it was said that dwarfs lived in caves there, and no one liked to walk on the sunny hillside.

William's mother often warned him not to go wandering in the hills, and to beware of any strange thing that he saw for fear it was enchanted.

But William saw nothing at all, and he wasn't a bit afraid of dwarfs, no, nor giants either. Not he!

One day he went to look for wild strawberries at the foot of the hills. They were hard to find but, just as he was about to give up, he suddenly saw a sunny bank, just a little way up the hill, where he was quite certain he would find some. To get there he had to cross a very boggy piece of ground – and dear me, before he knew what was happening he was sinking right down in it!

Quickly, William slipped off his heavy boots, which were held tightly in the mud, and leaped lightly to a dry tuft of grass.

"Bother!" he cried. "I've lost my boots! I shall get thorns and prickles in my feet if I'm not careful."

Then he saw a strange sight – for on a flat dry stone just in front of him there was a pair of smart red shoes with silver buckles! William stared at them in surprise. Who could they belong to? He looked around but he couldn't see anyone.

"Hello! Is anybody about?" William shouted loudly. "Whose shoes are these?" But there was no answer at all.

William looked at the shoes again. It seemed a pity not to borrow them when he had none. He wouldn't spoil them – he would just wear them home and then

try to find out who the owner was.

So he picked up the shoes and slipped them on his feet. They fitted him exactly.

William thought they looked very nice. He stood up and tried them. Yes, they really might have been made for him!

"I'd better go back down the hill," he thought suddenly. "I've come too far up, and Mother always warns me not to."

He turned to go back down – but to his surprise his feet walked the other way! Yes, they walked up the hill, instead of down!

William couldn't believe it. Here he was trying to walk down the hill and he couldn't. He tried to force his feet to turn round but it was no good at all! They simply wouldn't!

"Oh no!" said William. "Why did I meddle with these shoes? I might have guessed they were magic! I've got to go where the shoes take me, I suppose. I wonder, though, if I could take them off."

But his feet wouldn't stop walking long enough for him to try, so on he had to go. Up the hill his feet took him, along a steep path, and up to a small yellow door in the hillside.

As he came up to it, the door opened and a little dwarf, dressed in red and yellow, looked out. He grinned when he saw William.

"Ha! My shoes have caught someone at last. Good!"

"You've no right to lay traps like that," said William, crossly, as his feet took him through the door. "Take these shoes off my feet at once!"

"Oh, no, my fine fellow!" said the

dwarf, chuckling. "Now I've got you, I'm going to keep you. It's no good trying to get those shoes off – they're stuck on by magic, and only magic will get them off!"

"Well, what are you going to do with me?" asked William.

"I want an errand-boy," said the dwarf. "I do lots of business with witches, wizards and giants, sending out all sorts of spells and charms, and I want someone to deliver them for me."

"I don't see why I should work for you!" said William. "I want to go home."

"How dare you talk to me like that!" cried the dwarf, flying into a rage. "I'll turn you into a frog!"

"All right, all right!" said William, with a sigh. "But I shall escape as soon as I possibly can."

"Not as long as you've got those shoes on," said the dwarf, with a grin. "They will always bring you back to me, no matter where you go!"

Poor William. He had to start on his new job straight away.

The dwarf wrapped up a strange little blue flower in a piece of yellow paper and told William to take it to Witch Twiddle. The shoes started off at once and, puffing and panting, William climbed right to the top of the hill where he found a small cottage, half tumbling down. Green smoke came from the chimney and from inside came a high, chanting voice. It was the witch singing a spell.

"Come in!" she called when William knocked at the door. He went inside and found Witch Twiddle stirring a big black pot over a small fire. She was singing strings of magic words, and William stood open-mouthed, watching.

"What are you gaping at, you nincompoop?" said the witch, impatiently.

"I'm not a nincompoop!" exclaimed William. "It's just that I've never seen boiling water send up green steam before!"

"Then you are a nincompoop!" said the witch. "What have you come here for anyway?"

"I've come from the dwarf down the hill," said William. "He sent you this."

He held out the little yellow package, and the witch pounced on it greedily.

"Ha! The spell he said he would give me! Good!" William wanted to sit down and have a rest, but the enchanted shoes walked him out of the cottage and down the hill again.

Trimble the dwarf was waiting for him with a heap of small packages to deliver.

"Look here!" said William, firmly, "I'm not going to take all those. I want a rest."

"Well, you'll have to do without one,"

said the dwarf. "I want these packages delivered. This goes to Wizard Castaspell, and this to Dwindle the dwarf, and this to Rumble the giant."

"But I don't know where they live," said William.

"That doesn't matter," said Trimble. "The enchanted shoes will take you there!"

And so they did. It was most peculiar. First they took him to a little wood, in the middle of which was a very high tower with no door. A neat little notice said: CASTASPELL THE WIZARD.

"That's funny," said William looking all round. "There's no way to get in!"

He knocked on the wall of the tower.

"Come in, come in!" cried a voice.

"How?" asked William. "There's no door."

"Oh, bless me if I haven't forgotten to put the door back again!" said a grumbling voice from inside. "Come back, door!"

At once a bright-green door appeared in the tower.

William stared at it, astonished. Then he opened it and stepped into a small, round room where a hunched-up old man sat reading an enormous book. His beard was so long and thick that it spread all over the floor. William had to take care not to tread on it.

"Here you are," said William. "It's a parcel from Trimble the dwarf."

William gave the old man the package and left. To his surprise the door vanished as soon as he was outside. It was most peculiar.

His enchanted shoes would not let him stay for a moment. They ran him out of the wizard's wood and took him halfway down the other side of the hill before they stopped.

"What's the matter now?" wondered William. "I can't see any house. These shoes have made a mistake. I hope they won't keep me out here in the cold all day!"

Just then the earth began to shake beneath his feet! He felt frightened, and wondered if there was an earthquake.

Then suddenly he heard a cross little voice.

"Get off my front door! I can't open it. Get off, I say!"

The voice seemed to come from down below. William felt the earth shaking under him again and then, to his astonishment, he saw that he was standing on a neat brown trapdoor, just the colour of the hillside! On the trapdoor was a little nameplate that said: DWINDLE THE DWARF.

"I'm so sorry!" called William. There was an angry noise below. Then suddenly someone pushed the trapdoor open so hard that William was sent flying into the air and fell down with a bump.

"Careful!" shouted William, crossly. "You sent me flying!"

"Serves you right," said the bad-tempered dwarf, sticking his head out of the open trapdoor. "What do you want here, anyway? Are you the boy that brings the potatoes?"

"No, I am not!" said William. "I've been sent by Trimble the dwarf to bring you this package."

The dwarf snatched the parcel from his hand and disappeared down the trapdoor at once, slamming it shut behind him.

"Go away," he called. "And don't you ever stand on my door again."

At once William's enchanted shoes took him back up the hill at a fast trot.

"I've only got to go to Giant Rumble now," said William. "Thank goodness! I feel quite exhausted!"

Soon he came to something that looked like a big golden pole. As he got near it he saw that it was a long, long ladder of gold, reaching up into the sky and into a large black cloud.

His feet began to climb up the ladder, and dear me, it was very hard work! Before he was very far up he badly wanted a rest – but the enchanted shoes wouldn't stop. Up and up they went!

After a long while William reached the top. He looked round and saw an extraordinary palace, which seemed to be made entirely of mist.

"This doesn't look as if it is the home

17

of a giant," said William, to himself. "It's big enough – but it doesn't seem strong enough! It's all so soft and misty!"

But all the same, a giant did live there. The front door opened as William drew near, and inside he saw a great hall, higher than the highest tree he had ever seen. Sitting at a carved table was a giant with a broad, kindly face. He looked down smilingly at the boy as he walked forward. "Where do you come from, boy?" he asked.

"From Trimble the dwarf," answered William. "He sent you this parcel."

"About time too," said the giant, stretching out such an enormous hand for it that William felt quite frightened. "Don't be afraid, my boy. I won't hurt you. I'm a cloud-giant, and I live up here to make the thunder you hear sometimes. But I do no harm to anyone."

The giant opened the parcel and then frowned angrily. "The dwarf has sent me the wrong spell again!" he grumbled. "Do you know anything about spells, boy?"

18

"Nothing at all," said William.

"Dear me, that's a pity," said Rumble.
"I'm doing a summer-thunder spell, and
I've got to multiply twelve lightning
flashes by eleven thunder claps. I don't
know the answer. Trimble said he'd send
it to me, but he hasn't, I'm sure."

"What does he say the answer is?"
asked William, who knew his tables very
well indeed.

"He says that twelve flashes of
lightning multiplied by eleven claps of

thunder make ninety-nine storm-clouds," said Rumble.

"Quite wrong," said William. "Twelve times eleven is one hundred and thirty-two."

"Well, is that so?" said the giant. "I am pleased! Now I can do my spell. I'm really very much obliged to you. I suppose I can't possibly do anything for you in return?"

"Well, yes, you can," said William, at once. "You can tell me how to get rid of these shoes."

"Well, the only way to get rid of them is to put them on someone else," said Rumble. "Tell me who you'd like to put them on and I'll tell you how to get them off!"

"I'd like to make that horrible little dwarf Trimble wear them, and send him off to the moon!" said William.

"Ha, ha, ha, ha!" laughed the giant. "Best joke I've heard for years! That would serve him right. Now listen. Wait till the dwarf is asleep, and then slip these tiny stones into your shoes. You

will find that they come off at once. Put them on Trimble's feet before you can count ten, and tell him where to go. He'll go all right! The shoes will start him walking and he'll never come back."

"Oh, thank you," said William, gratefully and took the small pebbles that Rumble gave him. He said goodbye to the kindly giant and then climbed quickly down the ladder.

He was soon back at Trimble's house and found him having his dinner. The dwarf threw the boy a crust dipped in gravy and told him that as soon as he had finished eating there were some more errands to do.

"I'm going to have my after-dinner nap," he said, lying down on a sofa. "Wake me when you've finished cleaning up."

William was too excited even to eat his crust. As soon as he heard Trimble snoring loudly William slipped the magic pebbles into the shoes. They came off as easily as could be, and in great delight he ran over to Trimble. As soon as the shoes were off, William began to count.

"One-two-three," he counted, as he began to slip the shoes on to Trimble's feet – but to his horror the dwarf's feet were far too large – twice the size of William's! Whatever could he do?

"Four, five, six, seven, eight, nine—" he continued to count in despair, for the shoes certainly would not go on the dwarf's feet. And then, at the very last moment William had an idea. He would put them on the dwarf's hands!

He fitted them on quickly, counting "Ten!" as he did so – and at the same moment the dwarf awoke!

"What are you doing?" he cried angrily, jumping up. "I'll turn you into a frog, I'll—"

"Walk to the moon!" shouted William, in excitement – and then a most extraordinary thing happened! For the dwarf suddenly stood on his hands and began to walk on them out of his cottage!

Trimble was even more astonished than William.

"Mercy! Mercy!" he cried. "Take these shoes off."

"I don't know how to," said William. "But anyway, it serves you right. Go on, shoes – walk to the moon and then, if the dwarf has repented of his bad ways, you may bring him back again!"

The dwarf was soon a long way off, walking upside down on his hands, weeping and wailing.

As soon as the dwarf was out of sight a crowd of little folk came running up to William. They were dressed in red and green tunics and had bright, happy faces.

"We are the hill brownies," they said, "and we've come to thank you for punishing that horrible dwarf. Now we shall all be happy, and you and your friends can walk safely up the hillside. Ho ho! Wasn't it a surprise for Trimble to be sent walking to the moon on his hands! That was very clever of you."

The jolly little hill brownies took William safely back home, and even

fetched his lost boots for him out of the bog into which they had sunk. And now William and his friends walk unafraid all over the hills, for the friendly brownies are about now and the nasty dwarfs have fled, frightened by the fate of Trimble.

As for Trimble, he hasn't even walked halfway to the moon yet, so goodness knows when he'll be back!

The Bad
Little Bunny

Once upon a time there was a little bunny called Koo. He was the dearest, softest, prettiest little bunny on all the hillside, and his mother and father were very proud of him. But he was terribly naughty. Nobody could think why, because all his brothers and sisters were very obedient little bunnies, and always did what they were told.

"Don't go out on the hillside until the sun has gone," Koo's mother would say to them all. "It isn't safe until then."

And they would rub their wet little noses against her soft sides and say, "No, Mother, we won't."

All except Koo. He wouldn't promise not to do anything, just in case he should find he wanted to do it after all. And his mother would suddenly look round and say, "Where's Koo?"

Nobody knew! He had slipped off along the dark little passage and up into the soft, fresh air of the hillside.

His mother would fetch him back and scold him, and tell him a big man would come and shoot him, but he didn't seem to care a bit.

But one day something happened to Koo, and I'll tell you what it was.

That morning, very early, he and his brothers and sisters and mother and father were all sitting on the grass, busily washing themselves. Koo finished first,

and he sat up straight on his hind legs and looked at the country which lay all around.

He had never been allowed to go any farther than a short distance round about his hole, but now he felt very curious to know what the world was like a bit farther off.

Away down at the bottom of the hill stood a wood, cool and green in its early summer dress. Koo thought it looked really lovely.

"Mother," he said, "may I go down there?"

"Good gracious no, whatever next!" said his mother in surprise.

"Why not, Mother? Why can't I go?" he asked.

"Because it's too far from our hole," said his mother. "You'd get lost, and then a man would catch you."

"What would he do with me?" asked Koo.

"He would cook you and eat you!" answered his mother.

"What does 'cook' mean?" asked Koo,

who never ate anything but raw grass.

"You'd be put into a big pot with water in, and hung over a fire till you got hotter and hotter and were ready to eat!" said his mother, getting tired of his questions. "It's terrible to be cooked, so I've heard. Now it's time to go in – and remember, all of you, never go down to the wood until you are big and strong enough to look after yourselves properly."

Now Koo felt quite certain that he was old enough to look after himself, and he longed to know what was down in that lovely, cool-looking wood.

"How nice it would be to lie there, hidden in the grass all day, instead of being down in our stuffy hole!" he thought.

And the bad little bunny waited until no one was looking – then off he went! He scurried down the hillside in the sunshine, his little bobtail gleaming white as snow.

At last he came to the wood. It was very cool, very shady, and very green. The grass tasted most delicious. Little shoots of bracken were growing up here and there, and Koo ate those too, and thought how silly his mother was to say he was not to leave his home.

"When I've had enough to eat, I'll lie down under that bramble bush," said Koo to himself. "It smells nice, and it will be lovely to sleep in the open air."

Soon he had eaten so much that he really couldn't nibble another blade of grass. He wriggled beneath the brambles and found a nice, soft, dry bed for himself.

"I wish the others were here," said

Koo, suddenly feeling a little bit lonely. "Mother was quite wrong about being caught and cooked. Why, I've not seen anybody at all except bees and butterflies. Caught and cooked indeed!"

Just at that moment there was a stir and a flutter somewhere nearby. And you'd never guess what the poor little bunny heard someone say.

"Cook Koo! Cook Koo! Cook Koo!"

Koo could hardly believe his ears! Cook

Koo? Cook him? how dreadful! Somebody must have seen him. Then his mother was right, after all! Koo lay still as still and listened.

There it was again, nearer this time.

"Cook Koo! Cook Koo!"

Koo dashed out from the bramble bush and fled, trembling, through the wood. He came to a low hazel bush and hid himself there. But there was somebody else near there, saying the same thing!

"Cook Koo! Cook Koo!"

Off went Koo again, as frightened as could be. But, oh dear! The wood seemed to be full of people telling each other to cook Koo. First one called it out, then another, and whichever way Koo turned he heard it.

"I don't want to be cooked!" he wept. "I'm only a wee bunny. Don't cook me, I want to go home!"

"Cook Koo! Cook Koo! Cook Koo!" said somebody in the trees nearby.

Then Koo suddenly saw the hillside he had scampered down earlier in the day! What a piece of luck! Up he went,

faster than he had ever scampered before, longing to reach home before anyone could cook him. And behind him he heard "Cook Koo" getting fainter and fainter.

His mother was waiting anxiously beside the hole, looking for her naughty little bunny. She was very glad to see him, and could hardly bear to scold him, she was so happy to have him again.

Koo told her all about his dreadful adventure.

"They kept calling out to each other to cook me!" he said. "Wasn't it horrible of them, Mother? If I hadn't run very fast indeed, they might have cooked me, mightn't they? I'll never be disobedient again, never!"

Koo didn't know what his mother was smiling at, but I expect you do. Wasn't he a silly little bunny to be frightened by the cuckoos! But still, he was never disobedient again, so his adventure did some good after all!

The
Yellow Trumpets

Once upon a time there were two little elves who lived in Fairyland and made trumpets. They made all sorts of lovely trumpets – big ones, little ones, long ones, short ones, white ones, red ones and blue ones.

They sold them as fast as they made them, because the baby fairies loved blowing them, and were always coming to buy them.

"One penny, please," said Flip, giving a brownie a red one.

All day long they sold them in their little shop, and when night came they shut the shop and sat down to make more.

Soon every fairy baby, little elf, and tiny pixie had a trumpet, and you should have heard the noise in the streets and houses of Fairyland.

Tan-tan-tara! *Tan-tan-tara*!

It was the baby trumpeters blowing their trumpets.

The older fairies didn't mind at first. They liked the babies to amuse themselves and have fun. They put up with the noise and laughed.

But one day Pinkle discovered a way to make a trumpet which made such a loud noise that any passer-by nearly jumped out of his skin when he heard it!

It was a large, wide, yellow trumpet, beautifully made. Pinkle was very pleased with it.

"Flip!" he called. "Come here, and see my new trumpet!"

Flip hurried to see it. Pinkle showed the trumpet to him, then hid himself beside the window.

When a gnome came hurrying by the window, carrying his morning's shopping, Pinkle blew his yellow trumpet loudly.

Tan-tan-tan-TARA! it went, right in the gnome's ear. He had never in his life

heard such a tremendous noise.

He jumped into the air in fright, dropped his basket of shopping, and went scurrying down the street as fast as he could, feeling quite sure that some dreadful animal was roaring at him.

Pinkle and Flip laughed till they cried.

"Let's show the trumpet to the babies!" said Pinkle. "They're sure to want one each, and we will charge them sixpence!"

"Oh yes," said Flip in delight.

"Then we will be so rich that we'll never need to make any more trumpets, and we'll go away and have a lazy time for the rest of our lives!"

So the two naughty elves showed the baby fairies their new trumpet, and told them what fun they could have frightening everyone.

The little fairies thought it was a lovely idea, and sounded like great fun, and so did the baby pixies. They asked Pinkle and Flip to make them each one, and agreed that they would pay them sixpence.

So the two elves set to work, and by the next day they had made twelve, and sold them all for sixpence each.

Then what a noise there was in the streets of Fairyland!

Tan-tan-TARA! Tan-tan-TARA!

The new trumpets nearly deafened everyone, and made people jump in fright.

"This won't do at all," said the King of the Fairies. "We must stop this. We don't mind the little trumpets, but these big trumpets are too noisy. Pinkle and Flip must not make any more."

So a message was sent to tell the two elves they must not make any more of the big yellow trumpets.

They were terribly disappointed. What a shame not to make any more, just as they were getting so rich through selling them! Oh dear, oh dear!

Pinkle and Flip talked about the message very crossly, and then Flip suddenly whispered something in Pinkle's big left ear.

"Let's go on making them and selling them anyway. We'll tell the customers to come at night, and no one will know. Shall we, Pinkle?" Pinkle nodded.

"Yes! We won't take any notice of their silly message. We'll make lots and lots more, and sell them every night when it's dark."

So when their little customers came to the shop, the naughty elves whispered to them to come and buy their yellow trumpets at midnight, if they really badly wanted them.

And night after night naughty little fairies and mischievous little pixies came creeping to Pinkle's back door, paid sixpence, and took away a trumpet.

Pinkle and Flip became richer and richer, and Fairyland became noisier and noisier.

At last the older fairies became really angry. They couldn't even sleep at night because of all the noise. But although they watched Pinkle and Flip's shop carefully every single day, they never once saw the elves sell one of those big

40

yellow trumpets that made such a dreadful noise. They couldn't understand it. Where did the trumpets come from if Pinkle and Flip didn't make them?

"I know what we'll do," said one of the fairies. "We'll go to Flip and Pinkle's shop, and search it from top to bottom. Then we shall know if they have been making the trumpets. If they haven't, we must look somewhere else! We'll go as soon as the shop is open tomorrow!"

Now, that night when a little elf came to buy a trumpet, he told them what he had heard, and the two naughty elves were terribly frightened.

They knew that if they were found out, they might be sent right away from Fairyland, and they didn't want that to happen.

"What shall we do, what shall we do?" cried Pinkle. "We've nowhere to hide the trumpets!"

Flip thought for a minute.

"I know," he said, "we'll hide them in the fields. Quick, bring as many as you can!"

The two elves hurried out to the fields, where a great many yellow flowers were growing.

"If we stick our trumpets into the

42

middle of these yellow flowers, no one will guess where they are!" said Flip. "Come on!"

And quickly he began pushing a big yellow trumpet into each yellow-petalled flower. They matched beautifully!

When all the trumpets were hidden, the two elves went back to their shop. It was just time to open it, so they unbolted the door.

In came the King of the Fairies, and told Pinkle and Flip they were going to search the house from top to bottom.

"Certainly!" said Pinkle politely. "Please do! You won't find a single yellow trumpet here!"

And they didn't. Not one! But just as they were going away again, feeling very puzzled, a pixie came running in.

"Come and see the lovely yellow flowers in the field!" he cried. "They are wonderful! We've never seen anything like them before!"

Off went everyone to see them, and Pinkle and Flip were taken along too.

But when the fairies looked at them carefully, they saw what made the flowers look strange and beautiful – they each had a yellow trumpet in the middle of their petals!

"So *that's* where you hide them, you rascals!" cried the fairies, and caught hold of Pinkle and Flip angrily. "Out of Fairyland you shall go!"

"No, no!" wept Pinkle and Flip miserably. "Please let us stay. We'll never, never, NEVER make big yellow trumpets again!"

Suddenly a fairy had a great idea.

"I know!" he cried. "Let's allow Pinkle and Flip to go on making their trumpets for these flowers! See how much more beautiful they are with the long trumpets in the middle!"

"Yes, yes!" cried all the fairies and pixies.

So it was settled. And from that day to this, Pinkle and Flip had to work hard to make the big yellow trumpets for the loveliest yellow flowers of the spring.

You have seen them often, for daffodils

grow in everybody's garden – and if you look carefully at them next springtime, you will see how beautifully Pinkle and Flip have made their yellow trumpets.

The
Magic Bicycle

Peter had a lovely new bicycle for his birthday. It was painted bright red with a yellow seat, and on the handlebars was a bright silver bell. It was a fine bell, and had a very loud ring. You should have seen everybody jump when Peter cycled up and rang it just behind them.

Peter went out on his bicycle every day after school, just before tea. It was great fun cycling up and down the lane, ring-ringing all the way.

But one afternoon a strange thing happened to Peter. He was cycling along whistling happily to himself, watching rabbits scamper along the grassy verge.

When he came to the little hill that ran down to the sweetshop at the bottom, he took both his feet off the pedals and had a lovely ride – but, do you know, when he reached the bottom of the hill the bicycle wouldn't stop.

No, it went on, all by itself without Peter doing anything to help it. He was so surprised.

"What a funny thing!" he thought. "What's happened to my bicycle, why is it going by itself? Ooh! It's going faster! My goodness, I hope we don't run into anyone."

On and on went the little red bicycle, with Peter holding on tightly. It went faster and faster, and Peter had to hold on tightly to his cap, in case it blew away.

The bicycle raced through the village and made everyone jump quickly out of the way. It nearly knocked over Mr Plod, the policeman. Poor Peter couldn't possibly say he was sorry because the bicycle didn't stop.

On and on it went, up hills and down hills, along the country lanes, past fields and farmyards. At last the little red bicycle ran into a village Peter had never seen before. It was a strange place. The

houses all looked like doll's-houses, and there was a farm exactly like Peter's toy farm in the bedroom at home, with funny wooden-looking trees standing in rows, and wooden-looking cows grazing in the fields.

And what do you think were in the

street? Why, toys, all standing about and talking to one another, or shopping busily.

"This must be Toy Town," said Peter to himself, in astonishment. "Perhaps my bicycle came from here and felt homesick suddenly, and raced back home."

In the middle of the street was a wooden policeman, holding up his hand to stop the traffic. The bicycle tried to get past – but the policeman grabbed the handlebars and stopped it. Off fell Peter, landing with a bump.

"Why didn't you stop?" cried the policeman, crossly. "Didn't you see my hand put out?"

"Yes, but my bicycle wouldn't stop," said Peter. "It won't do what I tell it to!"

"I don't believe a word of it," said the policeman, getting out his notebook. "Show me your bicycle licence, please."

"But I haven't got one," said Peter in surprise. "You don't need to have a bicycle licence where I come from – you only have licences for motor-cars and television sets."

"In Toy Town you have to have a licence for bicycles too," said the policeman, sharply. "You must come to the police station with me, and pay a fine."

"But I haven't any money," said Peter, quite frightened.

"Never mind," said the policeman. "You can pay your fine in chocolate money instead."

"I don't have any chocolate money either," wailed Peter. But it made no difference. The policeman took him by the arm, and marched him down the street.

Suddenly there came a great noise of shouting not far off, and a big brown teddy bear rushed by, carrying a little bottle of brightly-coloured sweets.

"Stop thief, stop thief!" cried a little wooden shopkeeper dressed in a stripy apron. And all the toys standing around in the street began to chase the teddy bear, but he jumped into a toy motor-car and whizzed off at top speed.

Two more toy policemen rushed up. "Who has another motor-car that we can use to chase him?" they cried. But nobody had. Then Peter had an idea.

"I'll go after him on my bicycle!" he said. "Jump up behind me, policemen, and I'll scoot after that naughty teddy."

In a second he was back on his bicycle, and behind him crowded the three wooden policemen, and another teddy bear who wanted to join in the fun.

Peter pedalled as fast as he could, and soon he could see the teddy bear up ahead of him in the toy motor-car.

The teddy looked behind him and saw that he was being chased. He went faster still, but Peter pedalled as hard as he could and soon he had nearly caught up.

Suddenly the clockwork motor-car the teddy was driving began to run down. It went slower and slower, until finally it stopped. The teddy got out to wind it up again – but before he had given it more than one wind, Peter had pedalled alongside.

The policemen jumped off and grabbed the naughty teddy. They made him give up the bottle of sweets and said he must clean the whole sweetshop from top to bottom to show that he was sorry.

"Well," said the wooden policeman who had stopped Peter when he first arrived in the little village, "that was a very good idea of yours, to let us chase that teddy on your bicycle."

"That's quite all right," said Peter. "I was glad to help."

"Thanks very much anyway," said the policeman. "I won't say any more about your not having a bicycle licence. You can go home now – but please be sure to have a licence if you come to Toy Town again."

"Thank you," said Peter, sitting down on the grassy roadside. He was very hot and tired after his long cycle ride. "It's been a great adventure. But I do wish I didn't have to cycle all the way home again. This bicycle of mine won't seem to go by itself any more, and I shall have to pedal it up all of those hills."

"Dear me, I didn't think about your being tired," said the policeman, very much upset. "Look here, get into this

car with me – the one the teddy used.
You can put your bicycle in the back.
Can you drive a car?"

"No," said Peter, "not even a toy one,
I'm afraid."

"What a nuisance," said the policeman.
"I can't drive either." Then the clever
policeman had a wonderful idea.

"Hey, Teddy Bear!" he cried to the
miserable bear who was still being
marched off down the road. "You can

drive this car, can't you? You can do something else useful to make up for all the trouble you've caused."

"Oh! Yes," said the bear, pleased to show how clever he was. "Jump in everyone, and I'll drive Peter all the way home, if he will tell me where he lives."

Off they all went, right through Toy Town and back to the village where Peter lived. How his friends stared when they saw him drive up with three wooden policemen and two teddy bears – but before they could ask them any questions the toys had driven off again, and Peter was left standing by his gate with his little red bicycle.

"What an adventure," he said. And it certainly was, wasn't it?

Hazel's Umbrella

Hazel had a new umbrella. She was very proud of it, for it was a pretty green, and looked lovely when it was put up. She did wish it would rain – but the days were fine and sunny, and it seemed she would never be able to use it.

"Go into the garden and pretend it's raining!" said her mother. "You can have a nice game like that."

So off went Hazel. She looked up at the sky. "Dear me!" she said. "I think it's going to rain! I must put up my umbrella!" She put up her big umbrella. "It is pouring with rain!" she said. She was only pretending, but she really felt as if the rain were pouring. "What a good thing I have my umbrella, or I'd be wet through!"

She walked down the garden to the lilac bush, which she liked to pretend was her house. "I shall go indoors," she said. "But I'll leave my umbrella out to dry. It is so wet."

She left it open on the grass, and went under the lilac bush, pretending to take off her hat and coat. Soon she heard a funny little chattering noise, and she ran out from the bush. The noise was coming from her umbrella. How strange! Hazel

peeped around it – and saw four little brownies hiding underneath! They thought it was a tent and had come to live in it!

"Mummy, there are brownies hiding under my umbrella!" cried Hazel. "Come and see!" But before Mother reached the lilac bush, the brownies had gone! They were scared and ran into the flower-beds.

"I wish I'd seen them!" said Mother. I wish I had too – don't you?

The Night the Toys
Came to Life

The playroom was very, very quiet. Sarah and Jack had gone to bed. All their toys were shut up safely in the big toy-cupboard. It was dark in the room, and nothing could be heard but the ticking of the cuckoo-clock on the wall.

The cuckoo-bird suddenly popped out of the clock, flapped her wooden wings, and cried "Cuckoo!" twelve times. It was twelve o'clock, the middle of the night.

Now, one toy had been left out of the toy-cupboard, just one. It was Teddy, the big brown teddy bear. He had one glass eye, and one boot-button eye. Once he had lost a glass eye, so Sarah had sewn on a button instead, and he said he could see quite well with it.

Right now, Teddy was asleep, but the

cuckoo woke him up with a jump. "Who's playing hide-and-seek?" he cried.

The cuckoo laughed and popped her head out of the clock-door again.

"No one," she said. "I was cuckooing twelve o'clock, that's all. Teddy, you have been left out of the cupboard! Put the light on and let all the other toys out, and have a party!"

"Oooh yes!" said Teddy. So up he got, climbed on to a chair and switched on the light. Then he ran across to the toy-cupboard. He turned the key – *click* – and the cupboard door opened!

"Come out, toys, come out!" cried Teddy.

All the toys woke up with a jump. "Who is that calling us?" they cried. "Oh, it's you, Teddy. Can we really come out of the toy-cupboard? Oh, what fun!"

Then out came the curly-haired doll, very grand in a silky pink dress. Behind came the small teddy bear with his red hat and red jumper. Then came the jack-in-the-box, the little clockwork mouse, and the clockwork clown, tumbling head over heels. Two toy motor-cars came next, and then all the skittles, hopping on tiny legs. The skittle ball went with them, but he behaved well, and didn't knock the skittles down.

The pink cat and blue dog came together. They were great friends. The little train puffed out, and ran all round the floor in excitement. And Rag-Doll floated down from the top of the cupboard, hanging on to her parasol, so she wouldn't land on the floor with a big bump.

"Hurry, hurry!" said Teddy. "Don't

take all night walking out! We want to have some fun, and there won't be very much time."

"What shall we do?" said the curly-haired doll. "Let's do something really exciting! Shall we have a party?"

"Oh, yes, yes!" cried all the toys, and Teddy gave such a shout of delight that he quite frightened the clockwork mouse.

"I'll make some cakes on the toy stove!" said Teddy. "I'm good at that." And he set to work.

"Pink Cat and I will go to the toy sweet-shop," said the blue dog. "There are lots of sweets there. We will take some out of the bottles, and put them on little dishes. Everyone will like those."

"There is a jug of milk on the table," said the rag-doll. "I will get it, and we will fill the toy teapot with milk, and pretend it is tea."

Rag-Doll and Teddy got the jug safely down on the floor. The pink cat popped her head into the jug and took a lick. "Very nice and creamy," she said. "Oh, Teddy, how delicious your cakes smell!

Open the oven door and see if they are nearly ready."

The teddy opened the little oven door, and took out the pan of cakes. They were lovely – warm and brown, smelling most delicious.

"They are just ready," called Teddy.

"We had better dress ourselves up for the party," said the jack-in-the-box. "I shall put on a new hat and polish up my brass buttons a bit."

Everyone hurried to make themselves nice for the party. The curly-haired doll brushed her hair out till it was like a cloud round her face.

She tied it up with a blue ribbon. The pink cat got the blue dog to tie a bow round her neck, and she tied a blue bow round the blue dog's tail. He looked very smart.

Even the clockwork mouse got Small Bear to tie a sash round his fat little middle. "We want bows, too," said the skittles, but there was no more ribbon left.

"You look quite smart in your red uniform," said the clockwork mouse.

"Let's ask the doll's-house dolls as well!" said Teddy. "I am sure they would like to come!" So he knocked at the front door of the doll's-house, and the little mother-doll opened it.

She was so pleased when she knew there was to be a party. "I and Father-doll, and all the little children-dolls would love to come!" she said.

So they all ran out of the doll's-house

in their best dresses and suits, looking as sweet as could be.

"Now we will begin the party," said Teddy. "What shall we sit on? There are only two doll's chairs."

"We can each sit on a brick!" said the blue dog. "I will get them out of the brick-box."

The pink cat helped him to bring out the big wooden bricks, and they set them all round the little table. The curly-haired doll had already put a pretty cloth on it, and had arranged all the cups and saucers and plates from the toy teaset.

She had filled the big teapot with milk.

"I want to pour out, I want to pour out!" said the clockwork mouse. But the doll wouldn't let him.

"You would spill the tea," she said. "Go and sit down like a good mouse."

Even the big rocking-horse rocked up to join the party. He chewed up four of Teddy's cakes in no time and he drank fourteen cups of tea – though really it was milk, of course.

"Your cakes are delicious, Teddy!" said the rag-doll, and the bear blushed bright red with pride. He looked quite funny for a minute, but he soon became his usual colour again. It really was a lovely party.

"Has everyone had enough to eat?" asked Teddy at last. "There isn't any-thing left – not even a sweet, and the teapot is empty. What shall we do now?"

"Play games and dance!" cried the blue dog. "Let's play catch! I'll catch you, Small Bear, I'll catch you!" The small teddy bear gave a squeal and ran away. The clockwork clown went head over

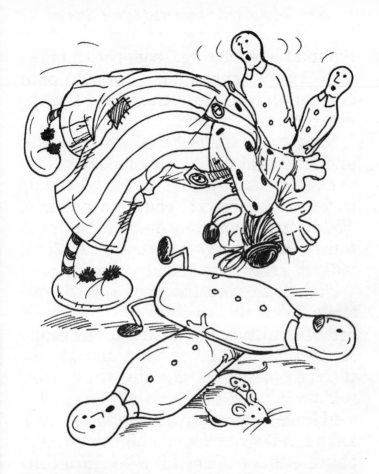

heels as fast as ever he could, and upset all the skittles.

Bang-smack-bang! Down they went with such a noise. The clockwork mouse squealed loudly when one skittle fell on top of him.

"I feel like singing," said the pink cat suddenly. "I want to sing." So she opened her mouth and sang loudly, but nobody liked her song at all.

"It's nothing but 'Miaow, miaow, miaow'!" said the curly-haired doll. "Do stop, Pink Cat."

"I want to dance!" cried a big skittle. "We skittles can dance beautifully. We want some music."

"Well, start the musical box then," said Teddy. "I'll wind the handle. Are you ready?" And then the room was suddenly full of loud tinkling music as the teddy turned the handle of the musical box. What a noise there was!

Now, outside in the street, the night-watchman was doing his round, with his torch in his hand. He was shining it on to people's front doors to make sure they were fast-shut. He was a very good night-watchman indeed.

Suddenly he came to a stop. "I hear a strange noise!" he said. "What can it be? It is music playing! It is people squealing and laughing. It is somebody singing a

loud Miaow song. What a very strange thing to hear in the middle of the night!"

He listened for a little while, and then he made up his mind to find out what all the noise was about. "I am sure the people of the house are all in bed!" he said. "Ho! Who can it be making all this dreadful noise? I must certainly stop it."

Now the toys hadn't heard the night-watchman walking by outside, because they were making such a noise. Suddenly they heard a knocking at the window!

"Oooh, what's that?" cried Teddy in a fright. "Turn out the light, quickly!"

So the curly-haired doll switched off the light – and then, in at the window shone the night-watchman's torch. Oh, what a fright the toys got!

"Save me, save me!" cried the clockwork mouse and bumped into all the skittles and knocked them down, *clitter-clatter, clitter-clatter.*

"What's going on here?" said the deep voice of the night-watchman, and he climbed in at the window. He shone his

light all round the room. "What, nobody here but toys?" he said in great surprise. "Then what could that noise have been?"

"Please, it was us," said the teddy, in a very small voice. The night-watchman was so astonished when he heard the teddy speaking to him that he couldn't say a word.

"You see, we were having a party," said the curly-haired doll, and she switched on the light again. Then the night-watchman saw the remains of the party on the table. "Teddy baked some cakes, and the pink cat got some sweets from the toy sweet-shop," said the doll.

"Oh, what a pity I didn't come a bit sooner," said the big night-watchman. "I could have had a cake then. I get so hungry in the middle of the night."

"I'll make you some!" cried Teddy, hurrying to the toy stove. "Have a ride on the rocking-horse while the cakes are baking. They won't take long!"

So the night-watchman got on to the rocking-horse, and the horse gave him a ride while the cakes were cooking.

The teddy bear baked a beautiful batch of cakes. The pink cat filled a little dish with more sweets from the shop. The curly-haired doll tipped up the big jug and filled the teapot once more. The doll's-house mother-doll took a cup and saucer and plate into the doll's-house and washed it for the night-watchman.

Suddenly something happened! The kitchen cat came creeping in at the door, for she had heard all the noise too. She stood there looking at the busy toys – and she suddenly saw the clockwork mouse rushing across the floor!

"A mouse, a mouse!" she mewed, and she pounced on the frightened mouse at once. The mouse's key flew out of his side, and he gave a loud squeal.

"Let the mouse go!" cried Teddy.

"Bad cat!" shouted the clockwork clown.

But the cat would not let the poor little mouse go. Then the big night-watchman got off the rocking-horse and walked over to the cat. He took out his black notebook and a big pencil.

"I must have your name and address," he said to the surprised cat. "I must report you for cruelty to animals. See how you have frightened this poor little mouse!"

The cat fled away in fright. The toys crowded round the night-watchman. "Oh, thank you, thank you, kind Night-Watchman!" they cried.

"You are so kind," said the clockwork mouse, rubbing his little nose against the night-watchman's boots. "I wish you were my very own Night-Watchman. I do like you!"

75

"Come and eat my cakes," said Teddy. The night-watchman looked at them.

"Dear me!" he said. "I shall never be able to eat all those! Can't we ask someone else to come and share them with me?"

"Let's ask Sarah and Jack!" cried Teddy. "They are asleep, but we can soon wake them."

"You go," said the rag-doll. "Tell them we want them to share in our fun. They are nice children and have always been kind to us. It would be fun to share the party with them."

So the teddy went out of the door and tiptoed to the children's room. He climbed up on to the bed and pulled at the sheet. "Wake up," he said, "wake up. There's a party going on!"

Sarah and Jack woke up. They were surprised to see Teddy. "Have you come alive?" they said.

"Of course I have," said Teddy. "Do hurry up and come to the party!"

So the two children put on their dressing-gowns and slippers, and went

to share the toys' party. They couldn't help feeling very excited.

"Here they come, here they come!" said the toys to one another. "Hello, Sarah; hello, Jack!"

The two children walked into the room and were most surprised to see all the toys running about, and the skittles hopping, and the two motor-cars rushing over the carpet.

But they were even more surprised to see the big night-watchman. "Good gracious!" said Sarah, staring at him.

"What are you doing in our playroom in the middle of the night?"

The night-watchman told them. "I heard such a noise in here, and I came to see what the matter was," he said. "Then the toys kindly invited me to their party. But the teddy bear made so many cakes that I knew I couldn't eat them all myself and I suggested asking someone to share them. So he went to fetch you two."

"Oh, how lovely!" said Sarah. "Teddy, I didn't know you could make cakes. You never said a word about it!"

Teddy bowed low and went very red again. He couldn't help feeling very proud. "Please sit down on the floor," he said, "and I and the dolls will wait on you. It is a great honour to have you and the big night-watchman at our party!"

So the two children and the night watchman sat down on the floor, and all the toys waited on them. "Will you have a cup of tea?" asked the curly-haired doll, handing a full cup and saucer to Sarah. "It's really only milk," she said in a whisper.

"It tastes just like tea," said Sarah, and she drank out of the tiny cup.

"Will you have one of my cakes?" said Teddy, and offered a plate of his little brown cakes. The children thought they were simply delicious. They crunched them up at once and told the teddy bear that they had never tasted such lovely cakes before. This time Teddy went purple with pride, and the clockwork mouse stared at him in surprise.

"Did you know you were purple?" he asked. "You do look funny, Teddy."

The night-watchman ate a big meal too – in fact he ate twenty-three of Teddy's cakes, and a whole dish of sweets. He drank sixteen cups of tea, which was even more than the rocking-horse had had.

It was a lovely meal, except when the rocking-horse came too near and nibbled some of the night-watchman's hair off. That made him rather cross and he took out his notebook again. The rocking-horse was afraid of being asked to give his name and address so he moved away quickly.

"Now what shall we do?" asked Sarah, when they had eaten all the cakes and sweets. "We can't very well play games with you toys, because we are rather too big, and we should make such a noise."

"We will give a fine show for you!" said Small Bear. "We will set the musical box going, and the curly-haired doll shall dance her best dance. She really does dance beautifully!"

So the curly-haired doll danced her best dance to the music, and everyone

80

clapped their hands. Then the clockwork
clown showed how well he could knock
down all the skittles by going head-over-
heels, but the skittles were tired of that
and they chased the clown all round the
room. He got into the brick-box and the
skittles locked him in there for quite ten
minutes. That did make the children
laugh.

Then the two motor-cars ran a race
with the train and that was great fun.

They all bumped into one another and fell over at the end, so nobody knew who won. Then Small Bear stood on his head and waved his feet in the air. Everybody thought he was very clever.

"Can you do that, Night-Watchman?" asked Teddy.

"I don't know. I'll try," said the big night-watchman, and he got up. But he couldn't do tricks like Small Bear.

He soon sat down again, and mopped his head with a big red handkerchief. "I'd rather watch you do tricks than try them myself," he said. "Hello – what's this?"

The night-watchman and the children saw that the toy farm had suddenly come to life. It stood in a corner of the room, and nobody had thought of waking up the farmer, his wife, and animals. But they had heard the noise of the party, and now they were all very lively indeed!

"The ducks are swimming on the pond!" said Sarah.

"The cows are nibbling the toy grass," said Jack.

"The hens are laying little eggs!" said the night-watchman in surprise. "And look at those tiny lambs frisking about! There goes the farmer to milk his cows. Well, well, well – it's a wonderful sight to see!"

The toy farm-dog barked round the sheep. The toy horse dragged the toy farm-cart along. The toy pigs grunted and rooted about in their little toy sty. The children really loved watching everything.

"Oh!" said Sarah. "I have always, always wanted our toy farm to come alive – and now it has. Jack, isn't it lovely? Oh, do look – the farmer's wife is offering us a tiny, tiny egg!" So she was. The night-watchman and the two children took one each. They were very pleased.

Just as they were all watching the toy farm, a loud noise made everyone jump. It was the toy cockerel on the farm, crowing as loudly as ever he could:

"Cock-a-doodle-doo! Cock-a-doodle-doo! Cock-a-doodle-doo!"

"It's daybreak!" cried Teddy, in surprise. "How quickly the time has gone."

"It's dawn!" cried the curly-haired doll. "The sun will soon be up. Time for all toys to go back to the cupboard. Hurry now, hurry! We must not be alive after daybreak. Hurry, toys!"

Then what a rush there was for the toy-cupboard! The night-watchman and the children watched in surprise. The skittles hopped in. The clockwork mouse tore in at top speed. The clockwork clown went head over heels right into the back of the cupboard. The pink cat and blue dog ran together, their whiskers touching. Teddy quickly put the bricks into the box. The doll's-house dolls cleared away the tea things, and then ran to their house and shut the front door.

"Goodnight – or rather, good morning!" said Teddy, popping his head out of the cupboard. "So glad you came and shared our fun! Goodbye – and come again another day!"

"Well, that's all over," said Sarah, with a sigh. "Oh, wasn't it fun? Did you enjoy it too, Night-Watchman?"

"I should think I did," said the night-watchman. "Well, I must be getting back to my work, or somebody will be after me. And you two had better go to bed. I'll get out of the window. Goodnight!"

"Goodnight!" said Sarah and Jack. They watched the night-watchman get out of the window and then they went to the door. "Goodnight, toys," they said softly.

And out of the toy cupboard came a crowd of tiny voices, from the little growl of Small Bear to the squeak of the clockwork mouse. "Goodnight, Sarah and Jack, goodnight!"

Then Teddy poked his head out of the cupboard again. "It was all because you didn't put me away in the cupboard tonight that the party happened!" he said. "Leave me out again sometime, please!"

"We will!" said the children. What fun they'll have when they do!

Hi-Yi's Boot

Hi-Yi was a very smart gnome who lived in a fine little house in Tip-Top Town. He was always very well-dressed, from his feathered hat to his brightly polished boots.

He had a brother who lived in Slap-Dash Village, about six miles away, and he sometimes used to visit him. His brother's name was Hoy-You, and he was very proud of Hi-Yi and his beautiful clothes.

"Hi-Yi is coming to visit me soon," he would tell the people of Slap-Dash. "You wait and see how he is dressed before you order yourselves any new clothes. Hi-Yi is sure to be dressed in the latest fashion, and you can copy his suit when you see what he wears."

So the people of Slap-Dash watched and waited for Hi-Yi and thought him very wonderful indeed. They were glad when Hoy-You beckoned to them one day and told them good news.

"Hi-Yi is coming to tea with me this afternoon," he said. "You can all come to tea, too. Then you will see how my handsome brother is dressed."

All the people got out their best coats and dresses, polished up their shoes and boots and brushed their hats. Then they waited for four o'clock to come, when they could go to Hoy-You's.

At two o'clock Hi-Yi started out from Tip-Top Town, dressed up in his best. He had a red hat with a white feather, a red tunic with white buttons, and red gloves. On his feet he wore a pair of red boots that reached to his knees. Very grand they were, and polished so brightly that when Hi-Yi bent down to look at them he could quite well see his reflection in them.

On the way to Slap-Dash Village he met So-So the pixie and stopped to have a chat with him. That made him late and he thought he would take a short cut. But he missed his way, and before he knew what was happening he was sinking in a bog.

"Help! Hey! Help!" he shouted. But there was no one to hear him. He struggled and struggled and at last managed to get out. But, oh dear me, he had left one of his beautiful red boots behind him! He was dreadfully upset.

He cleaned the other on the long grass nearby, and then polished it up with his handkerchief. He looked in vain for the one he had lost – it had sunk right down into the mud.

"Well, I shall have to walk to Slap-Dash without it, that's all," said Hi-Yi. "It's a good thing I have some nice thick socks on."

Off he started again and just after four o'clock he came to Slap-Dash and made his way to his brother's house.

"Goodness, he's got quite a party on today!" said Hi-Yi. "I shall have to sit down all the time and try to hide my stockinged foot. Oh, I do feel dreadful!"

He slipped in at his brother's back door and greeted him as he stood in the kitchen seeing to the tea.

"You're late, Hi-Yi," said Hoy-You. "Go on into the parlour and I'll come in a minute. Everybody's in the garden just now."

"Hoy-You, could you lend me a—" began Hi-Yi.

"A handkerchief? Yes, you'll find one in

my top left-hand drawer," said Hoy-You. "Go and find it yourself, there's a good chap, and don't bother me any more, because I'm busy."

Hi-Yi didn't like to tell him that it was a boot he wanted to borrow and not a handkerchief. He went into the parlour and sat down on a chair, putting his legs under it so that his feet could not be seen. Presently, Hoy-You came bustling in with the tea, and called to his brother.

"Come on into the garden, Hi-Yi, we're having tea there today, it's so fine."

Poor Hi-Yi! He had to stand up and follow his brother into the garden. Everyone looked at him as he walked out, for they all wanted to see the latest fashions from Tip-Top Town. And the very first thing that struck their eye was that Hi-Yi was only wearing one boot!

"Fancy! That's a strange fashion!" they whispered to one another. "Only one boot! My, that would be a saving on shoe-bills, wouldn't it!"

To Hi-Yi's tremendous astonishment, nobody asked him why he was only wearing one boot. He thought that everyone was being very polite and kind, pretending not to notice he wasn't wearing two boots, and he decided to ask them all to tea with him the next week, to show that he thought them very kind. The people of Slap-Dash Village were delighted with the invitation, and they all accepted gladly.

"We'll hire Pixie Lightfoot's yellow omnibus," they said. "And we'll be at

your house at four o'clock exactly."

Hi-Yi set off home feeling very pleased. He hadn't felt a bit uncomfortable only wearing one boot, because nobody had said a word about it. He hadn't liked to ask his brother to lend him an odd boot to walk back in, for he didn't think Hoy-You had more than one pair.

The next Tuesday, at exactly four o'clock, Pixie Lightfoot's yellow omnibus rolled up, and all the folk of Slap-Dash Village jumped out – and oh, what a very peculiar thing! They all wore just one boot each! Nobody wore two boots – each had a boot on the right leg, and a good thick sock on the other. Hi-Yi couldn't believe his eyes.

He was wearing a new pair of boots, yellow with red tops, very smart indeed. He looked at his brother – yes, Hoy-You was wearing only one boot too. Whatever could it mean? He took Hoy-You into a corner and asked him.

"What are you all wearing only one boot for?" he asked.

"Well, what are you wearing two boots for today?" said Hoy-You, indignantly. "You only wore one last week, and we all thought it was the very latest fashion. So when you asked us all to come to tea with you in Tip-Top Town we thought we must be fashionable too, and we all put on just one boot. And it's very nasty and cold for the poor foot that's only got a sock on, I can tell you! It's a pity you're wearing two boots today, Hi-Yi. Everyone will be most disappointed. They thought they really would be in fashion today – and now it's all altered again, and you're wearing two."

Hi-Yi began to laugh. He laughed and laughed and laughed. To think that everyone in Slap-Dash was wearing only one boot instead of two just because he had lost one of his in the bog. Well, well, well! Ha ha ha!

But Hi-Yi was a kind little gnome and he didn't want to disappoint everyone. So what do you think he did? He went into his bedroom, and took off one of his boots. Everyone was delighted when they saw him come out with only one on.

"We were right! It is the fashion!" they said, and they all felt very proud of themselves indeed, and enjoyed the party immensely.

"Hoy-You!" whispered Hi-Yi, just before everyone went, "I must just tell you something before these people get colds in their left feet – tomorrow the fashion will be to wear two boots again!"

"Thank goodness!" said Hoy-You, whose left foot was like ice. "I'll be sure to tell everyone."

They all said goodbye and, when the last one had gone, Hi-Yi sat down in his

little rocking-chair and put his boot back
on. Then he roared with laughter again.
He laughed till he split his fine new tunic
– but he didn't care! Such a good joke
as that didn't often come his way!

The Brownie Who Thought
He Was Clever

Once there was a little brownie called
Bron who was hunting for lost treasure.
He knew a pot of gold was hidden on
Rainbow Hill, but he didn't know how
to get there. So he went to the Simple
Witch, and asked her the way.

"Go down that path," she said. "It
leads to hilly country. Cross as many hills
as there are legs on a spider, and you will
find a river. Row down the river for as
many miles as there are legs on a
butterfly. After that count as many oak-
trees as there are petals on a wild rose.
Climb the last one, and you will see a
hill where, if you dig, you will find your
pot of gold."

Bron thought her directions rather
strange, but he wrote them all down. He

said goodbye and went away, humming cheerfully, thinking he would soon find the gold.

Now, Bron was a nice little brownie, but, like a good many people, he thought he knew everything. For one thing, he felt sure he knew how many legs a spider had.

"I can't think why the Simple Witch didn't say cross six hills, instead of 'as many hills as there are legs on a spider'," he said to himself. "I suppose she thought it sounded clever! Anyway, they aren't very big hills. I'll soon be there."

When he had crossed six hills he stopped and looked for the river. There wasn't a sign of one anywhere! "The witch was wrong!" said Bron angrily, and ran all the way back to tell her so. But she laughed at him.

"It's you who are wrong," she said, and wouldn't say another word.

At that moment, a spider dropped down from the roof and swung just above Bron's nose. And oh dear me! Bron saw it had eight legs, not six. So he ought to have crossed eight hills. He did feel silly! He had felt so certain that spiders had six legs. He slipped quietly out of the witch's cottage.

Over the hills he went again, one, two, three, four, five, six, seven, eight. Then he looked around.

And there was the shining river! He ran down to it, and jumped into a boat. "I'm to row as many miles as the legs on a butterfly," he said. "Aha, Simple Witch, you won't catch me this time! A spider has eight legs, so a butterfly has eight too! That's eight miles I must row!"

He set off. It was a long way, and the eight miles seemed more like sixteen. His arms ached and his head was hot with the sun. But at last he had rowed eight miles, and he looked around for the oak-trees. But there weren't any!

"Is the witch wrong or am I?" thought Bron. "I'd better catch a butterfly and count its legs!" At that moment a white butterfly perched on Bron's boat, and he leaped forward to count its legs.

"Six!" he cried. "Six! And I've rowed

eight miles. Oh dear! Why didn't I count a butterfly's legs first? I thought for sure they would have the same amount as a spider. Now I've got to go back two miles, and I'm so tired!" Back he rowed for two miles, and sure enough, there were the oak-trees.

"Now I've got to count as many trees as there are petals on a wild rose," said Bron. "I'm going to pick a wild rose and see how many petals it has first!"

He jumped out of his boat and went to a wild rose bush. He picked the first rose he saw, counted its petals, and stuck it into his buttonhole.

"Four!" he cried. "Now I'll count four trees and climb the last one. Then I'll see the hill where the gold is hidden!" So he counted four trees and climbed the last. But there was no hill to be seen! Not a sign of one! Bron was very angry indeed.

"I counted the petals!" he cried. "So the horrid old witch is wrong! I'll go back and tell her so!"

He rowed back for six miles, and

crossed the eight hills. Then up the path
he went, and burst into the witch's
cottage. She was talking to another
brownie, and was telling him the way to
go to find the hidden gold.

"It's no good going!" stormed Bron.
"I've been, and it's all wrong! The witch
doesn't know." The witch smiled and
said nothing.

"Well, I'll see for myself," said the other
brownie, catching a spider and counting
its legs. "I'll come back tomorrow and
tell you how I got on. Goodbye!"

103

"I'll come back tomorrow too!" said Bron to the witch. "And perhaps you'll admit you are wrong when we both tell you!"

As he went home, his wild rose petals began to fall – one, two, three, four.

Next day Bron went to the witch's cottage. There was no sign of the other brownie.

"Aha!" said Bron. "Your directions were as wrong for him as for me! He can climb the tree and look for as long as he likes, but he won't see a hill anywhere!"

The old witch stirred her pot and said nothing. Presently she lifted her head and listened. Bron listened too. Yes, someone was coming. Who could it be? Perhaps it was the other brownie coming back to say he had been given the wrong directions too. The footsteps came nearer, and then Bron saw that it *was* the other brownie.

And he had got a pot of gold!

"Where did you get that from?" asked Bron in astonishment.

"From the Rainbow Hill, of course,"

said the brownie. "I crossed eight hills, rowed six miles, climbed the fifth oak-tree, and from there saw the top of the hill away in the distance. The rest was easy."

"Climbed the fifth tree!" said Bron. "But I climbed the fourth! Wild roses have four petals, not five, and the witch said 'Count as many trees as there are petals on a wild rose,' didn't she?"

"Yes," said the brownie, laughing. "But you must have counted the petals of a rose that was nearly over! The petals fall one by one, you know, silly! Dear me, and I thought you were so clever, Bron! Fancy not counting the petals of two or three wild roses, to make sure of the right number!"

Bron remembered how his petals had fallen as he went home, and he blushed red and looked at the Simple Witch.

"I beg your pardon," he said. "You were right, and I was wrong. I'm not as clever as I thought I was!"

"Nobody ever is," said the Simple Witch, and wouldn't say another word. And what I'd like to know is this: Would you have found the pot of gold or wouldn't you? I wonder!

A
Christmas Wish

Once upon a time there was a poor boy named Sam. He lived in the Far North in a little house made entirely of wood. He had four little sisters and four little brothers, all younger than he was. His father had died several years before, and Sam and his mother had to work very hard to get food for them all to eat.

They had worked hard all year and now it was nearly Christmas time. All the children were getting very excited. One day, they stopped to gaze at a brightly lit shop window.

"Look at the beautiful decorations!" cried Sam's youngest sister.

"Look at all the delicious food!" cried his twin brothers together.

"And, oh, look at all the lovely toys!"

cried a third brother. "Sam, shall we have toys and good things to eat this Christmas?"

"I don't know," said Sam. "They cost a lot of money, and it is as much as we can do to buy bread. But if I can buy you toys, then you know that I will."

Sam didn't really think he would be able to buy his brothers and sisters what they wanted, even though it was his own heart's desire. His mother had been ill for many weeks and could not work, so they had not been able to save any money for Christmas presents. Sam doubted that they would even have enough to buy some special food for Christmas Day – a turkey, perhaps, or a plump plum-pudding. But he was a cheerful little boy and didn't give up hope, so out he went to work every day with a smile.

As he was walking along, Sam planned what he would do if only he could save some money from his wages.

"I'd buy a beautiful scarf and some chocolates for Mother, and a toy each for the boys and girls," he thought. "And I'd buy some lovely food for all of us. How nice that would be!"

But Christmas came nearer and nearer, and still Sam had no money to buy anything. Try as he might, he couldn't seem to save even a penny and as the days ticked by he began to look worried.

At last Christmas Eve came, and Sam knew his little brothers and sisters would have to go without toys or turkey. He was very sad as he walked slowly home after his long day's work.

It was late and very dark, and the snow lay thick on the ground. Huge, feathery snowflakes fell softly against his cheeks, and he wrapped his coat more tightly round him, for it was cold.

He shivered as the snow seeped through his worn-out boots, making his feet feel like lumps of ice. Poor Sam! This was surely the most dismal Christmas he had ever known.

Suddenly there came a sound of sleigh-bells, and down the road glided a sleigh drawn by reindeer. It went past so quickly that Sam couldn't see who was driving it. But as the sleigh passed him, something dropped at his feet, blown there by the wind.

Sam picked it up and looked at it by the light of his lamp. It was made of soft red velvet, trimmed with white fur.

"It's a cap!" cried Sam. "The driver of that sleigh must have lost it in the wind. I'll see if he comes back for it."

But though Sam waited a long time, no one came, so at last he went home with the red cap in his pocket.

He was wet through with the snow, and his feet were frozen solid with the cold as he wiped his boots on the mat at home.

His youngest sister, Sarah, who had been tucked up in bed, ran to greet him with a hug and a kiss. The rest of the children were fast asleep.

"You must be freezing, Sam," said his mother when she saw him. "And look at your poor wet feet!"

"Yes," said Sam, sighing. "My boots are nearly worn out now. I wish I had a new pair!"

And whatever do you think! Just as he said that, his old boots flew out of the door, and a pair of brand-new ones flew in!

Sam stared in disbelief. His mother rubbed her eyes, and looked again and again – but it was true. There stood a pair of fine new boots.

"This is magic," said Sam. "But I wish you could have a pair of fine new boots as well, Mother dear!"

And almost before he had finished

speaking, in flew another pair of boots which landed right next to the first! The two stared at them in amazement.

"Well, well!" said Sam's mother. "This is certainly magic. But where is it coming from! Have you been speaking to pixies, my boy?"

"Oh no, Mother," said Sam. Then he suddenly remembered the red cap in his pocket, and he pulled it out. "Maybe it has something to do with this," he said, and told his mother how he had found it.

"It must be a wishing cap!" said Sam

joyfully. "Oh, Mother! We'll wish for toys and a turkey, shall we? And oh! I would like a nice warm fire to dry myself by!"

Immediately a great fire blazed up in the chimney, and Sam hurried over to it, laughing happily.

But his mother looked worried and took the soft velvet cap from his hands.

"Sam," she said. "This is someone else's wishing cap, not ours. The owner of it may be looking everywhere for it. We must give it back at once and not use it

to wish for more things for ourselves."

"But how do we find who it belongs to, Mother?" asked Sam.

"Well, you've only got to wish that the owner was here, and the wishing cap will bring him," she replied, handing the cap back to her son.

Sam knew she was right. It would be wrong to keep a wishing cap belonging to someone else. So he wished once again.

"I wish the owner of this cap was here," he said loudly.

And can you guess who, seconds later, was standing there in front of them? Why, there in the middle of the floor, stood Santa Claus himself! Sam and his mother could hardly believe their eyes.

Santa looked very surprised at first, but when he saw his red velvet cap in Sam's hands, he understood what had happened.

"So you found my hat!" he said, and he broke into such a loud and jolly laugh that it brought all the younger children running from their beds. How surprised they were to find Santa standing there.

"This is a piece of luck!" said Santa, smiling. "For I need my cap especially tonight. You see, when my sack of toys gets empty, I wish it full again!"

Sam stared at Santa Claus in delight. Fancy the wishing cap belonging to him! He gave it back with a smile.

"I'm sorry to say we got two pairs of boots and this warm fire by using your cap," said Sam. "I hope it hasn't done the magic in it any harm."

"Bless you, no!" laughed Santa. "It was splendid of you to wish to find the owner. Lots of people wouldn't have done that. But if you'd kept my cap for yourself, you'd soon have found that it brought you bad luck and unhappiness, instead of good fortune and joy. Thank you very much for giving it back to me. Now I must be off. I have a hundred thousand homes to visit tonight!"

Off went the jolly man, tramping out into the snow, and then Sam heard the sound of sleigh bells going down the road.

Next morning you should have heard the shrieks and shouts and squeaks and

squeals of joy in Sam's home! Everybody's stocking was full to the brim with the things they wanted most – and Sam had a huge pile of presents on his bed too.

His mother found a lovely red scarf and a purse full of money in her stocking

– and when she went downstairs she gasped in surprise. On the table lay the biggest turkey she had ever seen, a monster plum-pudding and plates full of mince-pies!

"Thank you, Santa!" she whispered. All round them were apples and oranges, sweets and chocolates, and in the far corner was a Christmas tree, hung with more presents. And who do you think was on the top of the tree? Why, a little Santa Claus dressed in red, smiling at all the happy children.

"Wasn't it a good thing I found that wishing cap!" said Sam.

"And wasn't it a good thing you found the owner!" said his mother.

"Yes!" chorused the children, dancing up and down in excitement. "Now we're going to have the best Christmas Day ever. Aren't we the luckiest family in the whole world?"

They all had a perfectly lovely Christmas after that, and when they were dancing round the tree in the evening, they suddenly heard a chuckling

laugh. It sounded just like Santa Claus!

But he wasn't anywhere in the room, and Sam thought it must have been the little Santa Claus stuck on the top of the tree.

I wonder if it was, don't you?

Bun and the Pixies

Elizabeth had been having a lovely picnic with her toys, but now it was time to go home. Off they all went, Teddy, Panda and Bun, a fat little toy rabbit with big furry ears.

After Elizabeth had put them back in the playroom, Teddy, Panda and Bun told the other toys all about their picnic. The little clockwork mouse listened – but it wasn't long before he started to giggle.

"What *is* the matter with you, Clockwork Mouse?" said Teddy, at last. "What's so funny?"

"It's Bun," he said, with one of his sudden giggles. "He does look funny, don't you think?"

"Why, what's the matter with him?" said Teddy, surprised. And when

Clockwork Mouse told them, the toys gave a cry of astonishment for Bun had lost his tail. It had completely disappeared! Bun screwed his head round and looked at himself.

"Oh dear! Oh dearie me! Where's my tail? I must have dropped it."

"You really must have a tail," said Teddy. "You look quite silly without one."

Bun's ears drooped flat on his head and his whiskers twitched. "Where could I have lost it?" he said sadly. "I didn't even feel it coming loose."

"Well, you can start by looking along the path we took to the picnic," said Teddy. "You'll probably find it there. Cheer up!"

There didn't seem to be anything else to do but go and look. So Bun set off by himself. Soon he came to the woodland path, and looked very carefully in the grass. But there was no tail there.

A robin called to him, "Hello, Bun! What are you doing?"

"I'm looking for my tail," said Bun. "Have you seen it?"

"No," said Robin. "But Prickles the hedgehog might know where it is. He passed this way a few minutes ago. I only hope he hasn't eaten it."

What a dreadful thought! Bun's ears went flat again. He hopped quickly down the path after the hedgehog.

"Prickles!" he called as soon as he saw him in the distance. "Have you seen my tail? I've lost it."

"Very careless of you," said Prickles. "You'll be losing your ears and your whiskers next."

"Don't say that," said Bun. "I was just asking if you'd seen my tail."

"No," said Prickles. "I'll look out for it. Would it be nice to eat?"

"No, certainly not," said Bun. "It
might make you ill."

The hedgehog went off to look for
something else to eat and Bun hopped on
down the path. But he couldn't see his
tail anywhere.

Then suddenly he heard somebody
singing. Who could it be?

He came to a big oak-tree and peeped

round it. Beyond lay a tiny dell, surrounded by tall foxgloves, and in the middle of them sat a small pixie. She was rocking a tiny pixie baby in a little silvery cot!

How Bun stared! He had never seen a pixie before. Never! How beautiful she was! And, oh, what a tiny baby! Why, it was as small as the smallest doll in the doll's-house.

Bun crept nearer. He poked his soft little nose between two tall foxglove stems and watched.

The pixie lifted the baby up and put it on her knee. Then she began to tidy the cot. First she shook out a tiny blanket made of cobwebs. Then she smoothed the cot's soft, fluffy mattress.

Bun watched. He suddenly flicked his ears up straight and glared. Yes, he glared! Then he squeaked very angrily indeed, and rushed straight over to the pixie and her baby. She looked up in alarm at the angry rabbit.

"Oh, whatever is the matter?" she said. "You gave me quite a fright."

"That's my tail!" said Bun, fiercely,
and he pointed with his paw at the fluffy
mattress. "That's my tail! And I want it
back right now!"

"Oh, dear!" said the pixie, hushing the
baby, who had started to cry in a high,
tinkling voice. "Is it really your tail? I'm
terribly sorry. I found it in the grass over

there – and it's such a soft, fluffy little thing, perfect for my baby to lie on. I couldn't possibly guess it was a tail."

"Well, it is," said Bun, looking a little less fierce. "It's mine. How do you suppose I felt without a tail? I felt dreadful. And all the toys laughed at me!"

"I'm so sorry!" said the pixie, and she held Bun's tail out to him. "You must take it back straight away."

Bun held his fluffy tail between his

paws. He was glad to have it back again. "Why, it smells of honeysuckle," he said in surprise.

"Yes, I hope you don't mind," said the pixie. "I put some special fairy perfume on it to make it nice for Baby. She had such a lovely sleep."

The baby suddenly put out her tiny arms to Bun and caught one of his ears. She pressed it against her rosy cheek, gurgling softly.

"Hold her for a minute," said the pixie. "I want to get something." And to Bun's surprise she put the tiny pixie baby into his furry arms. She had green eyes, as green as the grass, and tiny pointed ears. Bun thought she was the most beautiful little baby he had ever seen!

The pixie came back with a needle and thread – and a big pink silk ribbon. "I'm going to sew your tail on for you," she said. "And I'm going to tie this new pink ribbon round your neck, just to say thank you for being so kind to us."

"I'm sorry I frightened you," said Bun. "I was just so surprised when I saw you using my tail for a mattress. But your baby's so nice that I really don't mind a bit now."

The pixie sewed on the tail. Bun sniffed hard. "I do smell nice!" he said, pleased. "Thank you very much. And, oh – what a beautiful ribbon for my neck! None of the other toys have a ribbon as fine as this."

The pixie tied it round his neck in a beautiful bow. "There! You look a very smart rabbit indeed. I do hope you'll

come back and see us again soon, and bring some of your friends with you next time."

"Oh, yes please," said Bun, delighted. "I will bring Panda and Teddy too. They would love to see a pixie baby. I'm sure they would."

Then Bun looked up and was surprised to see that the sky was as pink as the ribbon round his neck. The sun was setting and it was time for him to go home.

"Well, I must go now. Thank you for finding my tail." And he scampered off, full of excitement. What a dear little baby! How nice and small and cuddly it had felt – and to think that soon he would be able to show her to the other toys! He gave an extra big skip and a jump because he felt so happy.

The toys crowded round him when he got back. "You've found your tail! Who sewed it on for you? Oh, Bun, you do smell nice!"

So Bun told them the whole story, and now the toys are longing to meet the pixie baby themselves. And whenever Bun smells his honeysuckle-scented tail, it reminds him of that tiny pixie baby in the foxglove dell. How I'd love to have seen it, too! Wouldn't you?

Christmas in
the Toyshop

Once upon a time there was a toyshop. It sold sweets as well as toys, so it was a very nice shop indeed.

All the children loved it. They used to come each day and press their noses against the window, and look in to see what toys there were.

"Oh, look at that beautiful doll!" they would say. "Oh, do you see that train with its three carriages – and it's got lines to run on too."

"Look at the rocking-horse. I do love his friendly face!"

"Oh, what a lovely shop this is! When we grow up let's keep a shop just like this one!"

Miss Roundy, the shopkeeper, liked having a toyshop. She liked seeing the

children and showing them all her toys, and she nearly always gave them an extra sweet or two in their bags when they came to spend their pocket money. So, of course, the children all loved her.

The toys loved her, too.

"Look – she found me a new key when mine dropped behind the shelf and couldn't be found," said the clockwork train.

"And she put a spot of red paint on my coat where some got rubbed off," said one of the toy soldiers. "She's very, very kind."

The toys liked living in Miss Roundy's shop till they were bought by the children. It was fun to sit on the shelves and the counter, and watch the boys and girls come in and hear them talk. And it was very exciting when one of them was bought, and taken proudly away by a child.

The toys didn't like Sundays as much as weekdays, because then the shop was shut, and nobody came to see them at all. They couldn't bear it when Miss Roundy took her summer holiday and shut the shop for a whole fortnight! That was dreadful.

"It's so dull," complained the biggest teddy bear, and he pressed his middle to make himself growl mournfully. "There's no one to see and nothing to do. Miss Roundy even pulls down the window-blind so that we can't see the children looking in at us."

And then Christmas time came, and the toys had a shock. Miss Roundy was going to close the shop for four whole days and go away to stay with her aunt. Oh dear!

"Four days of dullness and quietness and darkness," said the rocking-horse, gloomily. "Nothing to do. No one to come and buy us, or see how nice we are. Four whole days!"

A black monkey with a red ribbon round his neck spoke in a high, chattering voice. "Can't we have a Christmas party for ourselves?"

"It's an idea," said the rocking-horse, smiling. "Let's all think about it till Christmas comes – then we'll have a grand time in here by ourselves!"

The day came when Miss Roundy was going to shut the shop. She pulled down the big window-blind. Then she turned to the watching toys.

"I'm going now, toys," she said. "I shan't see you again for four whole days. Be good. A happy Christmas to you – and try and have a good time yourselves. Do what you like – I shan't mind! Happy Christmas!"

She went out of the shop and locked the door. The toys heard her footsteps going down the street.

"Happy Christmas, Miss Roundy!" said everyone, softly. "You're nice!"

135

And now they were all alone for four days. What were they going to do?

The toys did what they always did as soon as the shop was shut for the night. They got up and stretched themselves, because they got stiff with sitting so long on the shelves and counter.

"That's better," said the rag-doll, shaking out her legs one after another to loosen them.

The pink cat rolled over and over. "Ah – that was good," she said, standing up again. "I do love a roll."

The little clockwork train whistled loudly and the toy soldiers climbed out of their boxes and began marching to and fro. "Nice to stretch our legs a bit," they said, and then they scattered because the roly-poly man came rolling along, not looking where he was going, as usual.

"Look out," cried the captain of the soldiers, "you'll bump into the doll's-house! There he goes, rolling to and fro – what a way to get about!"

"Listen, everyone!" called the rocking-horse. "Let's talk about Christmas."

"When is it?" asked the big teddy bear.

"The day after tomorrow," said the rocking-horse. "I think if we're going to have a good Christmas ourselves we ought to make our plans now, and get everything going, so that we're ready by Christmas Day."

"Oh yes!" cried everyone, and they all came round the rocking-horse. What a crowd there was. All the little doll's-house dolls, and the other bigger dolls, the

skittles, the railway train with its carriages, and another wooden train, and the roly-poly man, and... Well, I couldn't possibly tell you them all, but you know what toys there are in a toyshop, don't you?

"Sit down," said the rocking-horse. And everyone sat, except, of course the things that could only stand, like the trains and the motor-cars and the balls.

"We shall want a party," said the rocking-horse. "That means we must have things to eat. We can take any of the sweets and chocolates we like, to make into cakes and things – Miss Roundy said we were to help ourselves."

"We can make the food," said the doll's-house dolls.

"We'll help," said the skittles, excitedly.

"We can cook on that nice toy stove over there," said the twin dolls. One of the twins was a boy doll and the other was a girl doll, and they were exactly alike.

"I think the pink cat and the black monkey could arrange a circus," said the

rocking-horse. "They'll have great fun working together on that."

"I'll do the Christmas tree," said the sailor doll. "We'll have presents for everyone under it! We'll play games afterwards, too."

"What a pity Father Christmas doesn't know about us!" said the roly-poly man. "It would be so nice if he came to the party."

"I don't suppose he'll be able to come," said the black monkey. "He's much too busy at Christmas time. Don't roll against me like that, Roly-Poly Man. You'll knock me over."

The roly-poly man rolled away and bumped into a row of soldiers. They went down on the floor at once. As they got up and brushed themselves down, they shouted angrily at the roly-poly man.

"Don't let's quarrel," said the rocking-horse. "People should never quarrel at Christmas time. It's a time to make one another happy and glad. Now – to your work, everyone – and we'll see what a wonderful Christmas Day we will have!"

The dolls and the skittles set to work at once. The doll with golden hair and the twin dolls took charge of the cooking. They got the little toy cooker going, and there was soon a most delicious smell in the toyshop – the cakes were baking!

There were chocolate cakes and fudge cakes and peppermint buns. There were little jellies made of the jelly sweets Miss Roundy sold. There was a very big iced cake, with tiny candles on it that the rag-doll had found in a box.

The baking and cooking went on all day long. The twin dolls had to scold the roly-poly man ever so many times because he would keep rolling against the golden haired doll just as she was taking cakes out of the oven.

Still, as you can see, there was plenty of everything.

"What a feast we are going to have!" said the rag-doll, greedily. "Oooh – fudge cakes – I'll have six of those, please, on Christmas Day!"

The sailor doll did the Christmas tree. He was very, very clever. He climbed right up to the topmost shelf, which Miss Roundy had decorated with evergreens, and he chose a very nice bit of fir.

"Look out!" he called. "I'm going to push it off the shelf." So everyone looked out, and down came the little branch of fir-tree, flopping on to the floor.

The sailor doll climbed down. He did a little dance of joy when he saw what a wonderful tree the bit of fir would make. He wondered what to put it in.

"If you'll get me out of my box, so that I can join in the fun for once, you can use my box," said the gruff voice of Jack-in-the-box.

The toys didn't really like Jack-in-the-box very much. He lived inside a square box, and when the box was opened he suddenly leaped out on a long spring, and frightened them very much. The sailor doll didn't really know if he wanted to get Jack out of his box.

"Go on – just this once," said Jack-in-the-box. "I promise to be good. I'll

143

perform in the circus, and be funny if you like."

So Jack-in-the-box was taken out of his box and he wobbled everywhere on his long spring, enjoying his freedom very much.

The box was just right for the Christmas tree. The sailor doll filled it with earth that he took from the pot that held a big plant belonging to Miss Roundy. Then he planted the bit of fir-tree in it.

"Now to decorate it!" he said. So he got some tiny coloured candles and some bright beads out of the bead-box, and some tinsel from the counter, and anything else he could think of – and dear me, the tree really began to look very beautiful!

"I can make a star to go on the top of the tree," said the teddy bear, and he ran off to find some silver paper.

"And now you're none of you to look," said the sailor, "because I'm going to pack up presents for you – yes, a present for every single one of you!"

144

The circus was practising hard. There were two clockwork clowns in the toy-shop, so they were exactly right for the circus. They could go head over heels as fast as could be.

"We want some horses," said the black monkey, who was very busy. "Pink cat, stop prowling round the cakes, and see how many horses you can find."

The roly-poly man said he wanted to be a clown, so the teddy bear made him a clown's hat, and let him roll about the ring, knocking people over. Jack-out-of-his-box jumped about and waggled his head on his long neck. He was really very funny.

The pink cat borrowed some horses from the soldiers and the farm. She led them down to the circus ring.

Noah arrived with his animals from the ark. There were elephants, lions, tigers and even kangaroos!

"It's going to be a grand circus!" said the pink cat. "Oh, hurry up and come, Christmas Day!"

Well, Christmas Day did come at last! The toys rushed to one another, shouting "Happy Christmas! Happy Christmas!" at the tops of their voices.

The railway train whistled its loudest. The big bear and the little bears pressed themselves in the middle and growled. The musical box began to play, and the rag-doll sat down at the toy piano and played a jolly tune.

Nobody knew she could play and they were all very surprised. So was the rag-doll. She hadn't known either and once she had begun to play she couldn't stop! So what with the engine's whistle, the bears' growling, the musical box's tunes and the piano there was a splendid noise!

The roly-poly man got so excited that he knocked over two of the horses, rolled on the monkey's tail and upset a jug of lemonade.

"Can't you stop rolling about and be still for a moment?" said the pink cat,

147

keeping her tail well out of the way.

"I can't stand still," said the roly-poly man, "because I've got something very heavy at the bottom of me. It makes me wobble, but not fall over. I really will try to be good – but if you were as wobbly as I am you'd find it difficult, too."

The black monkey suddenly appeared dressed up in white trousers and a top hat! He carried a whip in his hand. He cracked it and made everyone jump.

Then the pink cat appeared, carrying a drum. She beat it – *boom-diddy-boom-boom-boom.*

"The circus is about to begin!" shouted the black monkey and he cracked his whip again. "Walk up, everyone! The circus is about to begin!"

Boom-diddy-boom-diddy-boom! went the drum.

All the toys rushed for seats. The black monkey had arranged bricks of all sizes and shapes out of the brick-boxes for seats and there was room for everyone. The doll's-house dolls were allowed to be at the front because they were so small.

The skittles were so excited that they kept giggling and falling over.

"Quiet there! Settle down, please!" shouted the monkey. "Pink cat, sound the drum again – the performers are about to march in."

The circus began. You really should have seen it. The horses were splendid. They ran round the ring one way, and then turned and went the other way.

Then the clowns came on, with Jack and the roly-poly man. The roly-poly man rolled all over the place and knocked all the clowns over. Then the clowns tried to catch Jack, but they couldn't, of course, because Jack sprang about all over the place, on his long spring. The toys almost cried with laughter.

The elephants were cheered when they came in. They waved their trunks in the air and trumpeted as loudly as they could. The lions and tigers came in and roared fiercely. The kangaroos jumped all round the ring and the bears walked

in standing up on their hind legs.

All the toys clapped and cheered and stamped at the end, and said it was the very best circus in the world.

The pink cat and the black monkey felt very proud and they stood in the middle of the ring and bowed to everyone so many times that they really made their backs ache.

"Now for the tea party!" called the doll with golden hair. "Come along! You must be very hungry, toys – hurry up and come to the party!"

What a wonderful tea party it was! There were little tables everywhere. In the middle of them were vases of flowers that the dolls had picked out of the dolls' hats that Miss Roundy kept in a box on a special shelf.

The tables were set with the cups and saucers and plates out of the boxes of toy tea sets. There was a teapot on each, full of lemonade to pour into the cups.

The cakes were lovely. There were fudge cakes, peppermint buns, chocolate cakes, all kinds of biscuits, toffee sandwiches, jellies that wobbled like the roly-poly man and, of course, the Christmas cake with its candles was the best thing of all.

"We've put it on a table by itself, because it's so big," said the golden-haired doll. "I hope there'll be a slice for everybody."

It looked lovely. The rag-doll had decorated it with icing. Everyone thought that was very clever indeed.

The pink cat ate so much that she got fatter than ever. The captain of the soldiers lent the twin dolls his sharp sword to cut the cake. The roly-poly man rolled up to see them cutting it, and nearly got his head cut off!

When nobody could eat any more, and all the lemonade was drunk, the skittles cleared away. "We'll do the washing-up and put all the tea sets back in their boxes," they said. "The rest of you can play games."

So, while the skittles were busy, the toys played party games. They played blindman's-buff, and the blindfolded pink

cat caught the elephant out of the Noah's ark.

"Who can it be?" wondered the pink cat, feeling the elephant carefully. All the toys laughed, because of course, they knew who it was.

They played hunt the thimble, and nobody could see for a long time where the thimble was hidden. Then the sailor doll gave a scream.

"The captain of the soldiers is wearing it for a helmet – he is, he is!"

And so he was. He was sorry to give it up because he thought it was a very nice helmet indeed.

The train gave everyone rides, and so did the toy motor-cars. Even the aeroplane said it would fly round the room once with everybody. The musical box played hard for anyone who wanted to dance.

The roly-poly man made everyone laugh when he tried to dance with the rag-doll. He rolled about so much that he knocked everyone off the floor.

They were all having such a good time. Then suddenly they noticed that all the candles on the Christmas tree were alight!

"Oh, oh! It's time for the Christmas tree!" cried the toys, and they rushed over to it. "Isn't it pretty? Look at the star at the top!"

"Where's the sailor doll?" said the roly-poly man.

"Gone to fetch Father Christmas, he told me," said the rocking-horse. "Do you suppose he meant it?"

And then, would you believe it, there came the noise of bells!

"Sleigh bells! It really is Father Christmas coming!" cried all the toys, and they rushed to the chimney. "He's coming! He's coming!"

Down the chimney came a pair of boots – then a pair of red trousers – and then with a jump, down on the rug came a merry, white-whiskered fellow, whose red hood framed his jolly red face.

"Father Christmas! You've come, you've come!" shouted the toys, and they dragged him to the tree.

"Wait a bit – I want my sack. It's just a little way up the chimney," said Father Christmas. So the big teddy bear fetched it. It was a nice big bumpy-looking sack.

"Happy Christmas, toys," said Father Christmas. He was a very nice little Father Christmas, not much bigger than the dolls. The toys were glad. They would have been rather afraid of a great big one.

"Happy Christmas!" sang out everyone. Then Father Christmas undid his sack. Oh, what a lot of things he had! There were ribbons and brooches for the dolls, sweets for the soldiers, chocolates for the Noah's ark animals, and balls, made of red holly berries, for the toy animals. Nobody had been forgotten. It was wonderful.

Father Christmas handed out all the presents, beaming happily. Then he took a few presents from under the tree.

"These are special presents for the

people who tried to make your Christmas so nice," he said. "Presents for the golden-haired doll and the twin dolls – and for the black monkey and the pink cat – here you are, special little presents for being kind and good."

"But what about the sailor doll?" said the rocking-horse, at once. "He did the tree, you know. Have you forgotten him?"

"Where is he?" said Father Christmas.

Well, dear me, he wasn't there! Would you believe it?

"I saw him last," said the rocking-horse. "He said he was going to fetch you, Father Christmas. Didn't he fetch you?"

"Well, I'm here, aren't I?" said Father Christmas, and he laughed. "Dear me – it's sad there's no present for the sailor doll, but I don't expect he'll mind at all."

The toys had opened all their presents. Somewhere a clock struck twelve. Midnight! Oh dear, how dreadfully late!

The twin dolls yawned loudly, and that made everyone yawn, too.

"We'd better clear up and go to bed," said the golden-haired doll. "Or we shall fall asleep on our feet, and that would never do."

So they cleared up, and in the middle of it all Father Christmas disappeared. Nobody saw him go. The pink cat said she saw him go into the doll's-house, but he wasn't there when she looked.

Somebody else was, though – the sailor doll! The pink cat dragged him out.

"Here's the sailor doll!" she cried. "Here he is! Sailor, you missed Father

Christmas – oh, what a terrible pity!"

But, you know, he didn't! He was there all the time. Have you guessed? He was Father Christmas, of course, all dressed up. He had climbed up the chimney when nobody was looking. Wasn't he clever?

"You were Father Christmas!" cried the golden-haired doll, and she hugged him hard. "You're a dear!"

"Yes, you are," shouted the rocking-horse. "That was the best part of all,

when Father Christmas came. We were so sad there was no present for you. But you shall have one – you shall, you shall!"

And he did. The toys threaded a whole lot of red holly berries together, and made him the finest necklace he had ever had. I wish you could see him wearing it. He does look pleased.

Miss Roundy will never guess all that the toys did in her toyshop that Christmas Day, will she? If you ever meet her, you can tell her. I do wish I'd been there to see it all, don't you?

A Tale of Shuffle,
Trot and Merry

"Now come along!" shouted Mr Smarty.
"Where are you, Shuffle, Trot and Merry?
I've some shopping here ready for you to
take to my house!"

They were playing marbles in a corner
of the market. Shuffle groaned. "Blow!
Now we've got to put his sacks of
shopping on our backs and walk for miles
to his house. I'm tired of it! Why doesn't
he buy a horse and cart for us to drive?"

"Because it's too expensive," said Trot.
"Come along – he'll be cross if we don't
hurry."

They went over to Mr Smarty, who
was standing by three big sacks.

"Oh, so there you are, you lazy lot!" he
said. "I've bought all these things at
the market, and I want them taken to

my house as quickly as possible."

"It's too hot to walk fast with big sacks like those!" said Shuffle.

"We won't get there before midnight," said Trot, gloomily.

"Well – I'll do my best," said Merry.

"I'll give a gold piece to the one who gets to my house first," said Mr Smarty.

They pricked up their ears at that! A gold piece! That was riches to them.

Sly old Shuffle went over to the sacks at once, and quickly felt them all. Oh, what a heavy one – and the second was heavy too – but the third one felt as light as a feather! That was the one for him!

"I shall hardly know I've a sack on my back!" he thought. "I'll easily be the first one there and I'll get the gold piece!"

He shuffled off with the very light sack on his back.

Trot went over to the two sacks left, wondering what was in them.

He stuck a finger into one. It was full of something round and hard – potatoes, perhaps? He stuck a finger into the other and felt something loose and soft. What was it – flour – salt – sugar? He pulled out his finger and sucked it. It tasted sweet and delicious.

"Ah – sugar!" he said. "Lovely! I can cut a tiny hole in the sack and dip my finger into the sugar all the time I'm walking along. What a treat!"

So Trot took the second sack and set off to catch up with Shuffle. Merry whistled a happy tune and went to the sack that was left. He made a face as he lifted it on to his back.

"It's heavy – full of potatoes, I think – probably covered in mud too, which makes them twice as heavy. Well, here goes, I must catch up Shuffle and Trot before they get too far, or I won't win that gold piece!"

But it was difficult to catch up with Shuffle, even though he was not the fastest walker as a rule, because his sack was so very, very light. Shuffle had no idea what was inside, and he didn't care. He was delighted to have picked such a light load!

"That gold piece is as good as in my pocket!" he thought. "And I'm going to keep it all for myself!"

Trot was having quite a good time with his sack, as he trotted along eating the sugar. What a joke, he thought – he was lightening his load and having a feast at the same time!

Merry walked fast, but his load was really heavy – and then he had the bad luck to stub his toe on a big stone, and that made him limp!

"Just my luck!" he groaned. "I'll never catch up with the others now. I can't walk fast with a sore toe!"

So Merry fell behind, but all the same he whistled a merry tune and smiled at anyone he passed. But soon clouds began to cover the sun, and a wind blew up and made the trees sway to and fro. Then Merry felt a drop of rain on his face and he sighed.

"Now it's going to pour with rain and I shall get soaked. I'd better give up all hope of getting that gold piece!"

The rain began to pelt down, stinging the faces of the three little fellows.

Shuffle was a great way ahead of the others, and he grinned as he looked round and saw how far behind they were.

But, as the rain poured down, odd things began to happen! First of all, Shuffle's sack grew heavier!

"Is my sack getting heavy, or am I just imagining it?" he thought.

He walked a little further and then felt that he must have a rest. "My sack feels twice as heavy! Whatever can be inside?" He set it down and untied the rope. He put in his hand and felt something soft, squashy and wet! The rain had gone right into the sack. Can you guess what it was inside?

It was a sponge! "No wonder the sack felt so light when the sponges were dry!" said Shuffle, in dismay. "Now they're soaked with rain and as heavy as can be! What can I do?"

Trot came along, grinning. "Hello, Shuffle. So your load was sponges, was it? It serves you right for picking the lightest load as usual. Now you've got the heaviest!"

"What's in your sack?" called Shuffle, annoyed, but Trot didn't stop. No, he saw a chance of winning that gold piece now. He was going quite fast. Also his sack felt lighter!

In fact, it soon felt so light that Trot stopped in surprise. "What's happening?" he thought. "My sack feels remarkably light!"

He put it down to see – and, to his horror, he found that the sugar was melting in the rain and dripping fast out of the bottom of the sack!

"I ought to get under cover, or it will all be melted away," thought Trot, in dismay. "Why didn't I remember that sugar melts? Well, I've outpaced old Shuffle – but if I wait till the rain stops Merry will be sure to catch me up and pass me, and I shan't get the gold piece."

So on he went in the pouring rain, while the sugar in his sack melted faster than ever. But at least he was now in the lead!

As for Merry he still whistled in the pouring rain, for he was a light-hearted fellow. The rain ran into his sack, down among the potatoes and soon muddy water was dripping out at the bottom. Merry laughed.

"You're washing all the dirty potatoes for me!" he said to the rainclouds above. "Hello – there's Shuffle in front of me. He's very slow today!"

He soon passed Shuffle, who groaned loudly as Merry passed him. "My load is sponges!" he shouted. "And they're four times as heavy as they were now that they're soaked with rain."

168

"Serves you right!" said Merry. "You picked the lightest sack so that you could win that gold piece!"

The three went on through the rain, and at last came one by one to Mr Smarty's big house. Trot arrived at the back door first and set down his sack on the ground.

"Hello!" said the cook. "Have you brought something for the master? I'll tell him you were the first to arrive."

The next was Merry with his sack of potatoes. The cook peered at them and smiled. "Well I never – the potatoes are all washed clean for me! That's a good mark for you, Merry."

Last of all came poor Shuffle, very weary with carrying such a wet and heavy load. He set his sack down and water from the sponges ran all over the floor.

"Now pick up that sack and stand it outside!" said the cook. "My floor's in enough mess already without you making it a running river. What in the world have you got in that sack?"

But Shuffle was too tired to answer. The cook gave them all some food and drink and they sat back and waited to be seen by Mr Smarty.

At last they were sent for, and the cook took them in to his study.

"Here's the one who arrived first," she said, pushing Trot forward. His sack looked limp, wet and empty. Mr Smarty glared at it in rage.

"What's this? It should be full of sugar!

170

Where's the sugar, Trot? Have you sold it to someone on the way?"

"No, sir. The rain melted it," said Trot, "I was here first, sir. Can I have my gold piece?"

"Bah! You don't deserve it," said Mr Smarty. "Why didn't you get under cover and save my expensive sugar?" Then he turned to Shuffle.

"Shuffle, you were third, so you're out of it. Take that disgustingly dripping sack out of the room. Merry, what about you?"

"Sir, he's brought potatoes – and they're all washed clean!" said the cook, eagerly, for she liked Merry. "He deserves the gold piece, even though he wasn't the first here!"

Merry laughed. "The rain did the cleaning!" he said.

"You weren't the first," said Mr Smarty, "but you certainly delivered my goods in a better condition than when I bought them – so I shall award the gold piece for that." He tossed a shining coin to the delighted Merry, who went happily off to the kitchen. What sulks and grumbles met him from Shuffle and Trot! He clapped them on the shoulder.

"Cheer up – we'll go and spend my gold piece together. What's good luck for but to be shared!"

They all went out arm in arm and the cook stared after them, smiling.

"You deserve good luck, Merry!" she called. "And you'll always get it – a merry face and a generous heart are the luckiest things in the world!"

I think she could be right.

The
Velvet Duck

The velvet duck lived with all the other toys. She had soft velvet wings, and a velvet back, with a red throat, a yellow beak and yellow legs and feet. She also had a beautiful voice that said "Quack!" very loudly when you pressed her in the middle.

Now none of the other toys had much of a voice. The teddy bear had only a very small growl because he had been pressed so often in the middle that his growl had almost worn out. Emma, the baby doll, once had a voice that said "Mamma", but when Sarah trod on her by accident one day, her voice disappeared. And the panda never had a growl or a squeak at all, though he pretended he had.

But of course, when the house was in darkness, and only the street light lit up the room, all the toys had lots to say! Their squeaks, growls and "Mammas" were only for the daytime – when day was gone they used their own proper little voices, and what a chatter filled the room!

Now it happened one evening that the velvet duck was feeling rather grand. Jack, the little boy the toys belonged to, had had a friend to tea. Sallie, the little friend, had liked the velvet duck best of all his toys. She had let the duck sit by her at teatime, and had made her quack a hundred times, if not more!

So no wonder the velvet duck was feeling pleased. Sallie had said that her quack was just like a real duck's and that she was the prettiest duck in the world. So the velvet duck was quite ready to be queen of the playroom that evening!

"Did you hear what Sallie said about me?" she said to the other toys. "She said my quack was—"

"Yes, we heard it," said the teddy bear, crossly. "We don't want to hear about it all over again. Forget it, Velvet Duck!"

"Forget it!" said the duck in surprise. "Why should I forget it? I don't want to forget it, I want to remember it all my life. Why, Sallie said I was—"

"Oh, do stop boasting!" cried the panda. "And don't start quacking, for goodness sake. We've had quite enough of that awful noise today."

"Well, I never! Awful noise indeed!" said the velvet duck, angrily. "Why, let me tell you this, Sallie said that I was the prettiest duck in the world."

"Well, you're not," said the curly-haired doll. "Sallie can't have seen many

ducks, or she wouldn't have said a silly thing like that. You're not a bit like a real duck. Not a bit! I've seen plenty of real ducks, and I know what they are like. You are a dreadful colour, and you have a terrible quack that we're all tired of hearing, so now please be quiet."

Well, the velvet duck was so angry to hear all that, that she hardly knew what to say. Then she quacked very loudly indeed and said, "So I'm not like a real duck, you say! Well, I am, so there! I can do everything a real duck can do. I wish

I was a real duck, so that I could live on the pond and not with nasty, horrid toys like you!"

"Can you lay eggs?" asked the teddy bear.

"Of course not," said the velvet duck.

"Well, a real duck can, so you're not like a real duck!" said Teddy.

"Can you swim?" asked the panda. The velvet duck didn't know. She had never tried.

"I expect so," she said at last. "I'm sure I could if I tried."

"Can you eat frogs?" asked the pink cat.

"Ugh, how horrible! I'm sure I don't want to!" said the velvet duck, feeling quite ill.

"You can't lay eggs, you can't swim, you can't eat frogs, so you're not a bit like a real duck!" said the teddy, laughing loudly.

"Ha, ha, ha!" All the others joined in the laughter.

The velvet duck turned red with rage.

"I tell you I am like a real duck, only

much nicer," she said. "I expect I could lay eggs and do everything else if I tried – but I've never tried."

"Well, try to lay an egg now," said Emma, the baby doll, giggling.

So the velvet duck solemnly sat down and tried hard to lay an egg. But it wasn't a bit of good; she couldn't. She was very disappointed.

"Well, eat a frog," said the panda.

"Get me one, and I will," said the velvet duck. But nobody knew where to find a frog, or how to bring it back to the room if they did, so they told the velvet duck they would take her word for that.

"Show us how you can swim," said Teddy.

"But where can I swim?" asked the duck. "There isn't a pond anywhere near, and the bathroom is too far away for us all to go there."

"You can swim in the tank belonging to the goldfish, up on that shelf there!" cried the curly-haired doll. She pointed to

where the four goldfish swam slowly about in a big glass tank of water.

But the velvet duck didn't like the idea of that at all! She shivered with horror at the thought.

"Oh, I don't think I'll try tonight," she said. "The goldfish might not like it."

"You're afraid!" cried the other toys. "You've told a story! You can't swim, Velvet Duck! You're not a bit like a real duck!"

This made the velvet duck so angry that she at once climbed up to the shelf where the glass tank sat. She perched on the side of the tank for a moment and then she hopped into the water. For a second or two she floated upright, and she was delighted.

"Look, look!" she called happily to the watching toys. "I can swim!" But, oh dear, whatever was happening? The water was soaking into her velvet skin. It went right through into the fluffy cotton wool she was stuffed with.

Poor Velvet Duck turned over and began to sink. How frightened she was –

and how frightened the toys were too!

"Help, help!" cried the poor velvet duck. "I'm sinking, I'm sinking! Help!"

The goldfish nibbled at her with their tiny mouths. The toys watched in horror. Whatever could they do? The curly-haired doll put her arm in the tank to try to reach her. But the tank was too deep.

Then who do you think came forward to help? The three little plastic frogs that Jack floated in his bath each night! They had sat as quiet as could be all through the quarrel, because they were only small toys, and didn't like to speak. Also they had felt rather afraid in case the velvet duck had offered to eat them instead of real frogs.

But they were brave, and they made up their minds to help. They jumped up on to the shelf, and leaped into the tank of water. They dived underneath the poor frightened duck and soon pushed her up to the surface again. Then Teddy and the curly-haired doll pulled her out. Dripping wet, she jumped down to the floor and stood there shivering.

"We're so sorry we teased you," said the bear, frightened.

"Do forgive us," said the curly-haired doll.

"I'm not like a real duck," said the velvet duck, sadly. "I can't even swim."

"No, but you can quack," said the panda, anxious to make everything right again. "Quack, duck, and let us hear your wonderful voice."

But what a dreadful thing! The water had got into the velvet duck's quack. She couldn't say a word. Not a single quack could she quack! She was upset. The water was very cold and she was shivering.

The toys were afraid she would catch a dreadful cold, so they took her near the radiator. Teddy took a fluffy blanket and wrapped it round the duck.

"This should keep you warm," he said.

The duck gradually got dry, but she was still sad.

"I've not even got my quack now," she said, with tears in her big glass eyes. "I can't swim, I can't lay eggs, I can't eat

frogs, I can't even quack. I might as well
be in the dustbin!"

"You mustn't say that!" said the toys,
shocked.

"Cheer up! We'll make you queen of
the playroom tonight, even if you can't
quack!" said the curly-haired doll, giving
her a hug.

And so the toys hurried around
gathering things for the party that night.

"We'll be the band," said the dominoes.

"I'll make the crown," offered the
curly-haired doll.

Soon everything was ready and the toys gathered round the velvet duck.

Teddy put the crown on Velvet Duck's head and all the toys clapped. But even that didn't make her feel very happy. She was so sad about her lost quack.

In the morning Jack came into the playroom to play. He said good morning to all of his toys and picked up the velvet duck. He pressed her in the middle, and guess what? Her quack had come back!

"Quack!" she said, even more loudly than before.

The water had dried out, and her quack was better than ever. The other toys were very pleased.

So now the velvet duck is very happy. She is still queen of the playroom and her quack is just the same. But there's one thing she won't do; she won't go anywhere near the goldfish tank, and I'm not surprised, are you?

The
Christmas Party

Donald was a lonely boy, for he had no brothers or sisters, and instead of going to school his mother taught him his lessons. So he had no friends and no one to play with. And will you believe it, he had never been asked to a party in his life!

At Christmas time he used to peep into other people's windows and see the children dancing round the Christmas tree and pulling crackers. He did so long to join them, but no one ever asked him.

One day, just after Christmas, Donald dressed himself up in the Wild West clothes that his mother had given him for Christmas. He looked very fine in the leather tunic, fringed trousers and enormous feathered head-dress. Just as he had finished dressing he looked out of the window and saw that there was a party next door. It was a fancy-dress party too! All the children that arrived were dressed up as fairies, clowns, milkmaids or soldiers.

"I'll go and watch them arriving," thought Donald. "That will be fun." So he slipped out of his front door and watched the children arrive. When they had all come he saw them playing games in the front room. So he went over to their front gate and watched.

Presently the door opened and a lady ran down to the gate. She took Donald's hand and pulled him to the door. "Here's a late little boy!" she called. "He's too shy to come in. Look at his beautiful fancy-dress!"

Donald tried to explain that he hadn't been asked to the party, but nobody listened to him. Soon he found himself playing musical chairs and pass the parcel, and then, dear me, he was sitting down to a most glorious tea! After that there was a conjuror who made a rabbit come out of Donald's tunic and two pennies out of his ears! Then there was a wonderful Christmas tree and Donald was given a fine trumpet and a box of chocolates.

All the other children liked Donald. He was full of fun, he didn't push or snatch, and he was just as ready to pass cakes at tea-time as to take them. The grown-ups liked him too, for he had good manners. As for Donald, he had never been so happy in his entire life.

But the loveliest thing of all was when

the prizes were given! Who do you think won the first prize for the best fancy-dress costume? Yes, Donald!

"But I can't take it," he said, "I wasn't asked to this party, really. That lady over there pulled me in. I'm only the little boy from next door, and this is the first party I've ever been to!"

"Well, of all the funny things!" cried the grown-ups. "We wondered who you were! But never mind, little boy, you deserve the first prize, so here it is – a railway train! And we hope you'll often come here and play with these children again."

Donald ran straight home with his prize, and his mother was astonished!

"I shan't be lonely any more!" said Donald. And you may be sure he wasn't.

Star Reads Series 2

Enid Blyton

Magical and mischievous tales from Fairyland and beyond....

978-0-75372-653-2

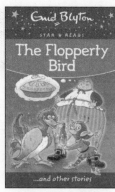

978-0-75372-652-5

978-0-75372-642-6

978-0-75372-651-8

978-0-75372-650-1

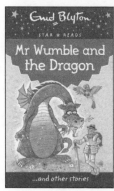

978-0-75372-649-5